•• THERE WILL BE •• WOLVES

There Will Be Wolves

Copyright ©2024 Anne J. Hill

Printed in the United States of America

Paperback ISBN: 978-1-956499-29-2

Edition one published in October 2024

Published by Twenty Hills Publishing

Edited by AudraKate Gonzalez, Beka Gremikova, Ellaina Ruse, and K.C. Lannon with help from Anne J. Hill and Moriah Chavis

Cover Art by Just Ventures Arts

Interior formatting by AudraKate Gonzalez and AJ Skelly

Content Warning: Fantasy violence, murder, physical, emotional, and verbal abuse, gore, violence against children

WOLVES

AudraKate Gonzalez
Anne J. Hill • AJ Skelly
Hannah Carter • Crystal Bailey
Rachel Lawrence • Brooke J. Katz
Maseeha Seedat • Morgan J. Manns
Nathaniel Luscombe • Miriam Wade
Mary Agnes Ratelle • Beka Gremikova
Ali Noël • Elaine Wells

PRAISE

"*There Will Be Wolves* is a collection of hair-raising short stories and heartfelt poetry perfect for fans of werewolf tales! There's sweet romance, friendship, vampires vs wolves, historical fantasy, and more! Some shifters choose to fight the monster inside of them, while others succumb to insatiable bloodlust. These stories remind me of the legend; we all have a good and evil wolf inside us fighting for supremacy. The one who wins is the one we feed." – J.R. Brady, Author in *Though We Bleed*

"From dark twisted tales of depraved monsters to the sweetest and goodest of boys, there's a little something in *There Will be Wolves* for everyone!" – Lacey R. Scott, Author in *Tails, Scales, & Tiaras*

AudraKate Gonzalez:
For all of those who were Team Jacob.
(I'm still Team Edward.)

Anne J. Hill:
For Lara and our blurry chats.

AJ Skelly:
For all the wolf lovers.

CONTENTS

THERE WILL BE WOLVES

BEKA GREMIKOVA

Listen to me closely, child
Listen to my cry
There will be wolves
Until the day you die

Clawing, gorging, feasting
Tearing up your flesh
There will be wolves
Who dare search out your death

But listen to me closely, child
All is not yet lost

There will be wolves
Who won't demand such a cost

Protecting, rearing, guiding
Lovers, friends—fierce, unrivaled
There will be wolves
Who will fight for you, my child

And one day you will realize
You've turned wolfish too
There will always be wolves
So protect the wolf in you

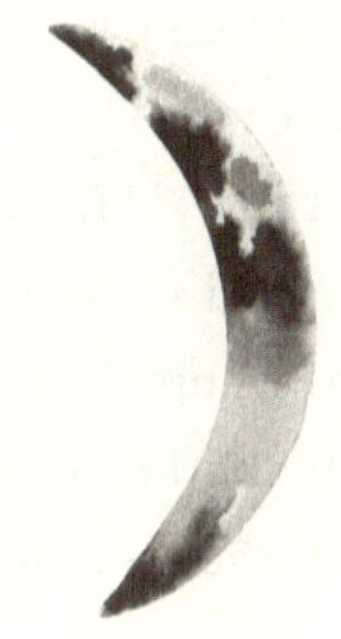

The Secret of Shifting

Maseeha Seedat

Hiro peeked open one eye at the sound of the creaking floorboards, the living room golden in the setting sun's light. Dark strands of hair distorted his vision, but through the curly locks, Hiro clearly saw his twenty-year-old roommate, Conan, frozen with his fist closed over the door handle. Hiro's breath hissed between his teeth, and he was pretty sure he heard Conan whisper, "Please don't wake up." Hiro groaned slightly, feigning a slow waking from his fake nap on the couch. This hadn't been Conan's first disruption of the evening, and Hiro was somewhat impressed he had managed to sleep through his roommate's antics the last few months. So far, Conan had tripped over the upturned edge of the living room rug, and even knocked his shin on the kitchen table. It was about time Hiro "woke up."

He stretched his arms wide over his head until his t-shirt lifted above his navel, then rubbed his eyelids sluggishly.

"Sorry about that," Conan said, his hazel eyes creased in apology. "I didn't mean to wake you."

"It wouldn't be the first time," Hiro said, holding back a fake yawn. His roommate chuckled at the hint back to when Conan had brought home a stray puppy in the middle of the night a few weeks back. Hiro didn't bother to look more alert. If Conan thought he was still tired, the older boy would never suspect Hiro of following him.

"Where are you going?" Hiro asked, though he didn't expect a straight answer. Their two-year age gap meant constant baby treatment from Conan . . . including frustratingly vague answers to most of his questions.

Conan adjusted the empty-looking duffel bag on his shoulder. "Gym."

"Oh, I'll come with you then."

"It's late—"

"The sun just went down." Hiro rolled his eyes.

"You have homework to do, though."

"Exams just finished." Hiro pulled himself out from under the blanket. "I'll do it next week."

As Hiro tried to stand, Conan shoved him back onto the couch, throwing the blanket on top of him. "Then chores." He smiled at Hiro's scowl. "The dryer's almost done and it's your turn to take out the garbage." Conan's fist trembled, a sure sign he was lying. He always shook out his hands when he lied. "I'll be back late, so don't wait up for me, 'kay?"

Hiro didn't bother fighting any further. He lay back down, snuggling under the blanket. "Fine. Have fun."

Hiro waited a few minutes after Conan locked the door to fling off his blankets and leap to his feet. They had only been roommates since the new semester started, but they had been friends long before then. Only after they moved in together did Hiro notice Conan's weird habit of disappearing for a few nights every month, each time leaving before sunset and returning the next morning with the first rays of dawn. Even if Conan could easily beat up anyone who bothered him, Hiro was worried for his safety. Maybe even just a little curious about his friend's weird tradition. Whatever his motive was, Hiro was sure he would discover Conan's secret tonight.

He pulled on his hoodie and running shoes, grabbed his phone, and slipped out of the apartment.

It didn't take long for him to catch up to Conan, who was—not surprisingly—walking in the opposite direction of the gym. Hiro followed from a distance as the sidewalks emptied out the farther they walked from the city center. Dense, bustling streets gave way to quieter neighborhoods until they had abandoned the city altogether for the vast, silent fields along its edges. The last orange hues had set by now, the sky's pale blue darkening as the full moon rose just below the clouds.

They were completely isolated. There was no point in hiding any longer.

"Conan Lincoln MaGallon!" Hiro yelled, shattering the silence. "You've got five seconds to explain yourself!"

Conan spun around, eyes wide. "Hiro— What are you doing? You have to leave!"

Hiro started running to close the distance between them. "If it's safe for you, it's safe for me."

"I never said it was dangerous." Conan's limbs lengthened in the moonlight, dark fur crawling down his arms. "Just get out of here!"

Hiro stumbled back. Out of all the reasons he had thought up for Conan's disappearance, arm-growing was not one of them. "Wh-what are you talking about?"

Conan's ears grew pointed. He huffed out a breath that almost sounded like a low growl. "Please, I don't want you to see me like this—"

Hiro's breaths quickened, and he struggled to hear Conan over the pounding heartbeat in his ears. "What . . . What are you?"

"I'm a werewolf, all right?" Conan's nose widened into a snout. "You have to go, please!"

A werewolf . . . Despite his fear, Hiro took a shaky step forward. Conan was his roommate. His best friend. A werewolf too, apparently, but did that really have to change things? "Don't chase me away, Conan." No more vague answers. No more beating around the scary—or more like furry—truth.

"You shouldn't be here—"

"I know you'd never hurt me. I'm not afraid of you." Hiro stood mere inches away from Conan, their height difference becoming increasingly obvious as Conan's legs began to grow too.

"It's not that!" A growl echoed in the wilderness. "I'm just . . . really dumb as a wolf. I don't want you seeing me chase my tail the whole night, okay?"

Hiro clutched his stomach and burst into laughter. "You . . . what?"

Conan arched his back, craning his head up towards the full moon. The last whiskers grew out of his snout before he turned full wolf and dropped to all fours.

Hiro wiped his eyes as if it could change what he saw. But, no, Conan was a full-blown wolf.

Hiro sat, crossing his legs. "It's okay, Conan. Come here." He held out his hand like he did to the stray puppy Conan had brought home. "You've looked out for me for a long time now. It's about time I pay you back."

Conan cocked his wolf head. His ears pricked up. Hiro tensed, fearing his best friend would bolt, and Hiro knew he couldn't keep up with a wolf. Conan sniffed out his palm, and Hiro yelped as the black bundle of fur barreled into Hiro. It wasn't long before the wolf was up again, switching between chasing his own tail or tussling with the back of Hiro's hoodie.

Hiro stood, laughing to himself as he began a moonlit search for a decently sized stick.

My Husband the Werewolf

Ali Noël

By day your name is Jim
Chances of homicide? Slim
But come night you snarl
And snap *my name's Carl!*
Before trying to bite off a limb

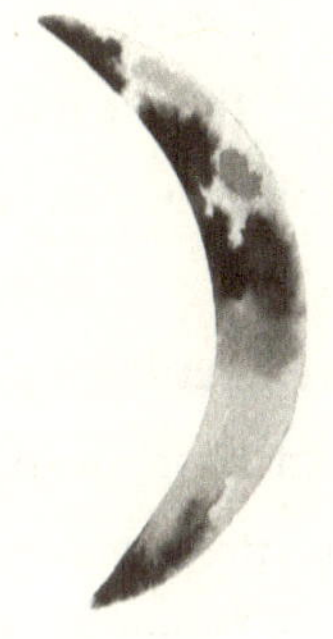

THE ACADEMY AND THE KISS

AJ SKELLY

FENNRICK

Who did after school projects on a Friday? I kicked the toe of my boot against the dirt path, bemoaning Etta's absence. Some Academy friends and a gaggle of female werewolves hiked beside me. Including Etta's cousin, Lexie, who couldn't keep her hands to herself.

It wasn't entirely her fault. At eighteen and next in line to be Alpha, my body was beginning to secrete its own kind of Alpha pheromones. They tended to drive the unpaired females into a sort of frenzy anytime they were around me.

It was exhausting being the only eligible wolf man.

Cariss smiled apologetically. She'd been the one to invite me after school with promises that Etta would likely be coming. But her sister's honey-blonde ponytail was missing.

"Fennrick," Lexie cooed. "Tell me more about becoming an Alpha." Her fingers fluttered near my arm. I resisted the urge to roll my eyes.

"Well, I'm taking a few classes for it this semester. Brushing up on diplomacy, leadership, that sort of stuff." I rubbed the back of my neck. I was trying to practice some of those diplomatic skills on Lexie. She didn't even go to Magik Prep Academy. Although she was thinking about transferring next semester. I really hoped my budding Alpha genes weren't the cause.

"But what's it actually like?"

Grueling, I thought. "Dad and I spend a lot of time together, which is nice. He's teaching me everything not covered in the books."

She smiled and batted her eyelashes.

"Fenn, did you catch the game last night?" Owen, an elf friend, attempted to save me.

"I did," I replied. Probably with more enthusiasm than I needed as I broke away from Lexie to walk beside him.

We hiked another half hour before the pulsating threads of magic surrounding Yggdrasil—the tree where all the magic in our world originated—thrummed in my chest. Yggdrasil was a popular destination. Touching the tree was forbidden but basking in its glow was encouraged.

We rounded the final bend and there Yggdrasil sat in all its glory. *Stunning*. I propped a foot against the low guard railing and took it in. An array of magnificent colors flew from its branches, tangling, weaving into the sky to form a multi-colored halo of magic around the tree.

Every time I visited, the awe was fresh. I closed my eyes and breathed deeply, the scent of pure magic washing over me and filling that aching tiredness inside.

"It's beautiful, isn't it?" Lexie said as she joined me at the railing. She'd stayed next to me the whole hike, peppering me with questions, scenting me frequently, though I don't think she knew I could tell.

I nodded.

"Fennrick, did you know my grandpa was an Alpha, too?"

I stared at her, confused where this conversation was going. She stepped closer, her arm brushing mine and sending the hairs on the back of my neck standing on end.

"Lexie," I started.

"Kiss me, Fenn. Seal our fate together here, beneath the most magical place in our world."

Shock dropped my mouth open as my eyes bulged in their sockets. She must have taken it as encouragement because she leaned in.

My brain froze. I did not want Lexie's lips on mine. She knew werewolf tradition dictated that I save any kisses for the one who would be the recipient of *all* my kisses, but my body was sluggish, refusing to move.

"Lexie!" Cariss grabbed Lexie's arm. "*What* are you doing?"

Lexie shot Cariss a murderous glare and yanked her arm away. But as she did, the back of her legs hit the low guard rail.

In stupefied horror, I reached to grab her before she fell, but I wasn't fast enough.

Lexie toppled right over the edge of the railing and hit the curling roots of Yggdrasil. Her scream pierced the air as her back smacked onto the roots and an amber glow immediately encased her.

Lightening cracked across the sky as a violent wind whipped through Yggdrasil's leaves, sending a rush of them over us. The colored threads of magic flickered and lost their curving waves, becoming jagged, harsh, and static.

Thunder boomed.

"Lexie!" Cariss shrieked.

The sky opened. Rain, hail, and flickering bits of magic sizzled onto the ground.

"We've got to get out of here!" someone shouted.

"What about Lexie?" Owen called over the din.

"We have to leave her," Cariss said. Terror clouded her face as her eyes met mine.

There was nothing we could do for her. We couldn't pull her back. The magical amber glow encased her completely. I glanced at Lexie's face.

Her eyes were rounded in shock, her mouth an unmoving gash of horror. Her hands were stiff, fingers splayed as if to catch her fall. Amber light pulsated over her prone form.

A leaf whacked into my cheek, breaking into my racing thoughts.

"Cariss is right. We have to go get help." The Alpha part of me took charge. "Go. Back down the path. Now." A forceful growl punctuated my words.

We'd just unleashed fury like our world had never seen.

We raced ahead of the storm, trying desperately to beat the roiling waves of magic and angry lightening back to the Academy—to warn the others, and find Headmaster Capra. If anyone would know what to do, it would be him.

"Move it, Owen!" Cariss shouted as gravel spun beneath the tires of his Jeep. The other cars followed as we sped far faster than was healthy down the back roads.

"No signal. Anyone else have a signal?" I asked as I jammed my finger over the home screen on my cell phone.

"Nothing," Cariss replied, a slight edge of hysteria in her voice.

Breaking all speed regulations, we were back at school within fifteen minutes. The magic that normally lazed dormant in the hallways like little strings of colored light, frizzed and sparked. Centuries-old magic rose from the stones like a thick cloud of dust.

Leaping from the car before it came to a complete stop, I flinched as screams echoed from inside. A young centaur burst through the double doors and galloped out of the parking lot.

"Go check in with the pack; tell Dad what happened," I ordered the rest of the girls as they pulled in. Without question they peeled back out of the parking lot.

"Etta!" Cariss shrieked as a honey-blonde head appeared.

My heart slammed in my chest. She was still here. Tatianna, Owen's girlfriend, came rushing out behind her.

"Cariss! Something's happened! The magic! It's unstable! Everything is changing!" Etta yelled as we covered the distance between the front doors and the vehicles. Etta's wide blue-green eyes were large in her face, her freckles standing out sharply against her pale skin. Her gaze flitted to me. My hands twitched to reassure her, though all I could offer were empty words.

"I know. I think it might be partly my fault," Cariss hiccupped. "Lexie's encased in Yggdrasil."

"*What*?" Etta said, dumbfounded.

"Come on." I ushered them back towards the building, surprised how the urge to take charge just came out.

"Tatianna, have you seen Professor Capra?" Owen asked, grabbing her hand. We quickly jogged back into the building where several students ran through the halls. Magic careened and dipped, smashing wildly into the stone walls, sending showers of spangles dashing into the air.

"Let's try his office." Tatianna's eyes sparked with her inner phoenix fire. She was on the edge of her control. We all were. Fur prickled under my skin.

Sprinting through the ancient halls, we dodged shards of magic. Busting around a corner, we were confronted with disturbing phantom-like shadows that wailed and scraped their ghoulish fingers towards us.

"What are those?" Etta gasped as I pulled her back around the corner, out of their reach.

"I don't know, but I don't think they're a natural phenomenon." My hand fell to the small of her back, herding her to the center and taking the outside edge of the group.

"They've got to be a product of this," Cariss batted a torpedo of neon magic out of the way, " magical insanity."

Owen jerked the door to the main office open.

"Duck!" he shouted as a swarm of wraith-like creatures flew over our heads, their shrieks deafening. Without thinking, I pulled Etta to my chest, curling myself over her like a shield.

"Go!" I pushed her into the office. Owen slammed the door shut behind us.

"Professor! Professor Capra?" Cariss shouted. Silence met us as we skidded to a stop before his ancient door inlaid with gold scrollwork.

We halted at the threshold. The hairs on the back of my neck stood on end as my werewolf senses tingled.

The door creaked open. Etta gasped.

"Professor Capra," Tatianna's whisper dropped into the heavy silence.

The professor stood in his doorway, his rotund belly stretching the gold buttons of his velveteen vest, his goat legs planted heavily on the floor. He gripped his cane. His whole body flickered. Like he was desperately hanging on to his corporeal form.

"The magic," The aged faun halted as his form shuddered in and out of visibility. "It is . . . taking us . . . old ones. Too much . . . magic . . . stored inside."

"What do we do?" The words sounded like my voice, though I wasn't sure I'd uttered them. Etta grasped my shaking forearm.

"You need . . . a unicorn." His body shivered violently and when it returned, he was completely transparent.

"Look . . . below . . ." He tapped his cane.

POOF!

With a wail that sent the group of us cowering, Professor Capra burst into a cloud of black and went screeching out the door, a phantom ghost himself.

"This is *so* bad," Tatianna whispered. Her eyes were fully enflamed, only *just* keeping her fire inside.

"A unicorn?" Cariss said.

Etta's hand was still on my arm. I clutched it.

"Nobody has seen a unicorn in a thousand years," Etta breathed.

We were screwed.

ETTA

Fennrick gripped my hand like it would keep him from drowning. Despite our heinous circumstances, it sent heat shooting to my middle. I *liked* the way his hand felt wrapped around mine. It gave me a fleeting feeling of security along with a wild rush of emotion. And then there was his smell. His mouth-watering scent. I knew it was his Alpha pheromones hard at work, but it was nearly enough to make me forget our dire situation. That and the fact that I'd wanted to be Fennerick's girl since I was thirteen, long before his Alpha genes kicked in.

"Where do we find a unicorn?" Owen asked, the tips of his pointed elf ears going as pale as the rest of his ashen skin. His question jerked me back to the present.

"What was it the professor said before he disappeared? 'Look below?' What does that mean?" Fenn asked the group.

"Look below," Cariss repeated, a crease forming between her eyebrows. "Below where?"

"Below, like below a bridge with the trolls?" Owen snorted.

"Below the ground?" Tatianna offered. She leaned into Owen, her inner fire going down to a simmer as he looped an arm around her shoulder.

"Below ground? Below ground where?" Cariss tapped her lip.

"What if he meant below the school?" I offered. The suggestion sounded ridiculous the moment it left my lips, and I felt my cheeks heat in response. Fenn looked at me.

"No. What if he *did* mean below the school. He tapped the floor right before he disappeared. Could there be a place *below* the school? We all know there are tunnels down there . . . but what if there's something . . . else?"

Cariss cocked her head to the side. "Well, the school is—what—a thousand years old?"

"No one has seen a unicorn in a thousand years," I murmured.

"Could that be a coincidence?" Fenn's fingers squeezed mine. A faraway look flashed through his eyes.

"Would the library still have original blueprints of the school?" he asked.

"Let's go look. We're not getting anywhere just standing in Professor's office," Tatianna said as she stalked towards the door.

The ancient Gothically arched hallways were eerily silent as we made our way to the library. The students racing around earlier were either gone or had hopefully made it to safety. Even the wraith-like creatures were gone. Erratically flickering bits of magic were the only noises as they hissed and popped in the top-most cracks and crevices of the arches.

The library doors were open, just like on any normal school day. The floor to ceiling bookshelves were crammed with everything from ancient scrolls to modern day paperbacks.

"In the resource room?" Cariss shrugged.

"Good a place as any to start," Fenn replied. My skin tingled as he touched my back to move me in that direction. I needed to get a grip.

Dust and age-old magic ticked my nose, and I clapped a hand over my mouth to catch my sneeze.

"Bless you," Fenn whispered, still close to my side.

"Thanks," I sniffled.

"Where do we start?" Tatianna asked as we broached the resource room. Tall scrolls and heavy ancient tomes scattered the large room.

"Time for the wolves to come out to play." Fenn nodded to Cariss and me then wasted no time. He jerked his arms backwards, taking his shirt off in that way only guys do. I'd seen him shirtless countless times over the years growing up in the same werewolf pack. But his abs were a lot nicer now than they had been a few years ago.

Cariss elbowed me and I blushed to the roots of my hair.

"Right. The older the document, the mustier it will smell," I stammered, fervently hoping Fenn didn't notice. Cariss and I quickly ducked behind a heavy-laden bookshelf and shifted to our fur.

I sneezed again as spangles of warped magic tickled my wolf's senses. Following Fenn's instructions, we quickly put our noses to work. It wasn't long before we'd unearthed a stack of ancient scrolls tucked neatly away in a forgotten box. Scents of stale magic and aged parchment for the win.

"Hurry up and shift back, guys," Tatianna said as she poured over the scroll.

"I think this might be it. Look," Owen said excitedly.

Within a minute, we were back in skin and taking in the prints.

"It's like a labyrinth." I shuddered.

"Roll the prints up. We'll take them with us." Fenn nodded decisively. Owen carefully rolled the blueprints.

Minutes later, the five of us stood facing a heavy, iron-bound door at the end of a seemingly abandoned corridor deep in the belly of the Academy.

"I don't like this," Cariss whispered. I knew how she felt. Night had fallen. It was pitch black but for the occasional spatter of unhealthy magic and the glow of the one torch we'd been able to successfully light with fragmented strings of partially exhausted magic.

Fennrick reached for my hand. I didn't object.

"Tatianna, keep your flames close in case that thing goes out," Owen said.

"No problem with that," she replied, swallowing hard.

"I'm going in fur," Fenn said. "Carry my clothes?" he asked me. I swear a light blush stained his cheeks. I hoped he couldn't hear my heart rate pick up.

"Sure," I squeaked. He didn't need to explain that his wolf had better night vision and a better chance of defending us should it come to that.

Cariss opened the door.

A smell like wet death filtered up from the massive black hole before us. I shivered and Fenn's tail brushed against me.

"Let's go." Cariss' voice wavered.

Tatianna held the torch high. Fenn went in first.

The stones were damp and there was the occasional squelching noise that I refused to think too hard about. Deeper and deeper, we went into the ground. First through damp, brick arches, then into rough, hand-hewn stone passages.

"How old do you think this is down here?" Cariss whispered. I'd been wondering the same thing.

Fenn growled low in his throat, his ruff standing on end.

Wind whooshed up the rough corridor and sent my hair flying as a scream built in my throat.

A deep roar boomed up from the depths. Fenn planted himself in front of the group, his own deep warning echoing back and mixing with the echoes of the *thing* until it made my ears ache.

The torch flickered out and Tatianna screamed. Her eyes flashed once in the dark before a white-hot stream of lightening-like fire streaked from her eyes and illuminated the entire hallway.

A black apparition wavered in the dark shadows. My body froze, terror crawling over my skin like a hundred spiders.

"Light the torch, Tatianna," Owen commanded. "Don't char me in the process."

Breathlessly, we waited for the *thing*, listening, straining our senses. My hands gripped Fenn's clothes hard enough my knuckles cracked, and I wondered if I should shift to my fur, too.

Flames engulfed the torch, igniting frayed bits of magic as the fire burst onto the stone ceiling.

The apparition hadn't advanced. It wavered there on the outskirts of the torchlight.

Fenn growled low in his throat and scented the air. All I smelled was toasted magic and fear. Possibly my own.

"I don't think it's real." Owen whispered.

"You sure?" Tatianna said.

"If it were alive, I'm pretty sure your flame fest would have fried it. Look. I think it's just a magic illusion," Owen explained.

Fenn nudged me closer to Cariss with his tail, yipped at Owen, then stalked down the dark hallway.

"Be careful," I whispered.

I held my breath as Fennrick tracked down the hallway, his growls echoing off the stone walls. About halfway down the hall towards the floating black mass, his posture relaxed, and he trotted back to us.

He barked once and my shoulders relaxed.

"Not real then?" Owen confirmed. Fenn bobbed his head and met my eyes before jerking his head for us to move forward again. He brushed against my side as we went down the corridor, sending flutters into my middle while reassuring my jagged nerves.

The apparition disappeared the moment we stepped within a few feet of it. It was nothing but wisps of ancient magic, long forgotten by its creators.

We trudged on. After what felt like hours of wandering and multiple stops to consult the blueprints, we finally came to the deepest point marked on the prints. There was nowhere else to go. A solid door fitted with an iron latch stood between us and whatever waited on the other side.

Fenn nudged me and Cariss behind him again and nodded to Owen.

Grasping the doors as Tatianna's eyes flashed with ready flames, Owen pulled the latch. A loud *clink* echoed down the stone corridors. Goosebumps rippled down my skin.

The ancient door swung open.

Caked in dust, cobwebs, and strings of fluttering magic, the most majestic of all beasts stood solitarily in the middle of a tiny stone chamber.

A unicorn.

The golden horn was tightly wrapped with magic, though pieces of it hung in strips. Whole chunks of what appeared to be magic-spun cloth were sagging from its white form like ripped threads of a funeral shroud. Cobwebs stretched from the beard to the chest. Shiny, golden hooves were dull and brassy with age.

"Oh," Cariss gasped.

The nostrils flared. My heart slammed into my throat. Fenn's tail pressed against my leg as his lips pulled back from his teeth.

Ever so slowly, with a noise like cracking plaster, the eye lids fluttered, breaking free of their ancient crusts.

The creature shrieked and shook the dust from its coat.

The noise echoed in my chest and sent me cowering on the ground. My hands clapped over my ears; eyes and ears both smarting from the bits of magic flung from the unicorn. All of us huddled, in awe and fear, staring at the creature of legend before us.

"What has happened to the magic?" The unicorn's voice—rich like dark chocolate, smooth like velvet, and hard like diamonds—thundered in the tiny space.

We were too shocked to answer.

"What has happened to the magic?" the unicorn bellowed.

"A . . . a girl—a werewolf—fell onto Yggdrasil's roots." Cariss was the first to find her voice.

The unicorn snorted.

"We've no time to lose. Come."

The unicorn stamped his front hooves, the sound reverberating around us. In awe, we watched as the dirty hair and strings of magic fell away. The coat grew thick and shiny, the hooves and horn glowed with the inner magic of the unicorn.

"Wolf, you may change back. No harm shall befall you whilst in my company."

Fenn bobbed his head at the unicorn's words.

I gathered his clothes into a neater pile on the ground where I'd dropped them then nudged them towards him and turned. He quickly shifted back, and I let myself sag a little in relief as he took my hand once he was back in skin.

The trip back through the twisty, winding underground took a fraction of the time with the unicorn confidently leading the way.

I was bursting with questions, but I didn't think it would be appropriate to barrage a creature so rare that it had nearly faded into myth. It seemed too irreverent.

Instead, I clung to Fenn's hand, trying not to think how much I was going to miss it and *him* once our world was righted. Assuming it *could* be fixed.

The hall was pitch black and deathly quiet as we crept from the belly of the earth.

"You may extinguish the torch."

Tatianna did as the unicorn told her. With a toss of its mane, light emanated from the unicorn.

"Have you any mode of transport that will take you quicker to Yggdrasil? In my day we'd have to round up some wild gryphons and magic them or make the journey on foot."

"We've got a Jeep," Fenn offered.

"A Jeep. What manner of beast is this? Some new hybrid, perhaps?"

"It's . . . a mechanical beast." Fenn rubbed the back of his neck.

The unicorn snorted. "All this magic and they still tinker with mechanics." The front doors of the school loomed ahead in the shadows.

"Please, sir, do you have a name?" Tatianna asked tentatively.

"I am Lazaren."

Tatianna quickly introduced each of us as we walked and exited the building. Wind and hail lashed around us as leaves and frazzled magic zinged and flew across the parking lot. Yet nothing touched us in the circle of Lazaren's glow.

"That thing is a Jeep?" Lazaren whickered in disdain as we reached the vehicle. "I shall meet you at Yggdrasil. See that you are not detained." With that, he broke into a gallop. Enormous white glossy wings edged in gold burst from the creature's back and he took flight, taking his inner light with him.

We were left again in darkness, suddenly caught in the uproar of the storm with his absence.

Yggdrasil was tempestuous—leaves stripped from its branches, magic gone but for a few bare tendrils stubbornly clinging to some odd twigs. Terror gripped me.

Lazaren stood beside the guard rail next to the glowing, amber encasement where Lexie must have gone over. I bit the inside of my cheek, realizing I didn't know what had happened to make her topple over in the first place.

Lazaren asked my question in his next breath.

"What transpired here?"

Fenn rubbed the back of his neck again and refused to meet my gaze. "She tried to kiss me," he started. My hackles rose, even in my human skin. I had no formal claim on Fenn, but Lexie wasn't even a member of our pack.

"It wasn't Fennrick's fault," Cariss interjected. "I tried to stop her. I grabbed her arm."

Had Fenn *not* tried to stop Lexie?

"She jerked back and tripped."

"And I wasn't fast enough to stop her," Fenn said, his voice strained.

"And when she hit the roots, the world fell apart." Cariss shrugged, her misery clear. I squeezed her arm, and she gave me a grateful, ghost of a smile.

Lazaren looked hard at each of us in the group. My skin tingled. Not in a bad way, but in an anticipatory sort of way.

Gingerly stepping over the guard rail, magic flared to life beneath his golden hooves as they touched Yggdrasil. It didn't spread, but illuminated Lazaren, and cast light back onto the pulsating, amber glow over Lexie.

"You tried to take something that does not belong to you," the unicorn said over the quivering amber. I was close enough I could see Lexie's eyes widened, though the rest of her body stayed still. "I will let you out, but until the wrong has been righted, the magic will not be reversed." He glanced back at us. "No one touch the magic or the tree."

Raising up on his back legs, Lazaren cried into the air and brought his flashing hooves down. Yggdrasil's roots quivered. "Let her go. I am here now," the unicorn said to the ancient tree. Yggdrasil groaned.

I shivered as beads of frantic magic skittered over my skin. With a pointed look at me that dropped my stomach to my toes, Lazaren wrenched his horn through the crust of swirling amber. A noise like thunder booming over the ocean echoed around us.

Without meaning to, I gripped Fennrick's hand. His fingers squeezed tight around mine.

Gasping and spluttering, Lexie sat up.

"Lexie!" Cariss said in relief.

"Phoenix, seal the gap once she's up," Lazaren instructed.

Tatianna nodded and Owen reluctantly let her step closer towards the barrier.

The unicorn prodded his horn at Lexie, and in a show of great humility on his part, let her maneuver herself up using his mighty horn as leverage.

As soon as Lexie had cleared her magic cocoon, Tatianna let her eyes blaze. Chills tickled my arms as the flames danced in her eyes before they shot out in a stream of white-hot fire over the gap in the amber crust. It sealed together like it was welded with lava.

Storm clouds still thrashed overhead, and magic and lightning lit the sky as they clashed together. Sparks flew and shattered on the ground. Fenn tugged me closer so that my arm brushed against his side.

"I . . . I'm so sorry," Lexie whispered brokenly against the gale that whipped the leaves into little funnels around us.

Lazaren stared at Fenn solemnly. "T'was you who was wronged, Wolf. You must right it."

Fenn's face paled, and his throat bobbled as he swallowed. Slowly he turned to me. Lightening flashed and showed me his hazel eyes, full of questions and hope.

"Etta," he rasped. My heart sped up. "Lexie tried to take what's rightfully yours. I mean, mine to give, but only for you to take."

Understanding dawned and my lips parted in surprise. Alpha pheromones flooded the air around us and my heart pounded in exhilarated expectation.

"You want *me*?" I whispered.

"Yeah. I really, really do." He smiled, though uncertainty crept into his eyes.

Tingling rushed through me as *rightness* settled over me. His hand dropped mine and tentatively grazed my waist.

A wave of heat crashed through me, and my answering smile stretched my face.

"Yes." I breathed the word.

Fenn's eyebrows crinkled as his eyes turned serious. Wind whipped hair into my face, but before I could move it, he nudged it aside and his hand cupped my jaw. Tilting my face, his lips closed softly over mine.

Literal sparks exploded around us. We jerked apart, startled, and watched as magic whirled in the sky and came streaming, rushing, swirling back to Yggdrasil. Leaves reeled from the ground back into the leafy boughs. Sunlight broke through the black clouds and bathed the ground in iridescent sparkles that came up and flitted around us.

Tatianna laughed as some of the sparkles landed in her hair and lit it up like a halo. The flames rose in her eyes and she let loose a stream of fire towards the rising sun, lighting a path straight over the top of Yggdrasil.

Fenn kissed the side of my head while we watched, but I turned and tugged his head back down for another, longer one.

He pulled me flush against him, his scent closing in around us. His smell slowly began to change, and I realized his hunt for the other half of his pair—for *me*—was over.

"Well done, children," Lazaren said. "You have saved your world, but if we do not return quickly to the school, without my stabilizing presence, so many different kinds of magic in one place will cause another explosion. I will not be able to save you should that happen."

We raced back to the Academy, magic swirling happily once more, though anxiety sat heavily with us. Lexie remained silent in the back seat. Lazaren again awaited us as we pulled into the parking lot and hopped out.

Relief was potent as I saw Professor Capra waiting at the double doors. He bowed low as Lazaren approached and we followed behind.

"Lazaren. Old friend. Thank you once again for your sacrifice." The old faun's horns were parallel to the ground as he used his cane to help him show his reverence.

"Capra." Lazaren inclined his head towards the professor.

"Children, follow me once more into the labyrinth."

We didn't dare question him, so we once more made the long trek into the darkness of the school's underside. Lexie trailed uncomfortably behind. It wasn't as scary this time with Lazaren's glow and with Fenn's fingers laced with mine. I sighed in contentment.

We reached the tiny stone chamber once more, the door still standing open.

Lazaren stopped just outside the door.

"You will be the next generation of leaders of this place. Capra will not live forever. Remember my existence."

And with that, he went in and stood in exactly the same spot and the same position as when we found him.

With a twist of his head, my mouth fell open as strands of magic wound around his horn, funneling over his sleek body, coiling and weaving together in a magnificent tapestry of swirling, sparkling magic.

Once the magic had encased his full body, he turned his face to us. He gave us a sleepy wink with one drooping eyelid, then he went still.

I squeezed Fenn's hand.

Our world was safe once more.

THE FROG WOLF

ANNE J. HILL

On a log, sat a frog
With dreams unheard of
Love beyond his being
For the princess he admired

A kiss turned the frog into a prince
She brought hope to his world
A vibrancy a frog could never know
His heart ready to soar

Naive
Passion

For the woman
Of the lunar

She kissed the prince and he turned
Into a shadow in the night

Claws and fangs
Under the crescent moon
His body shifts, snaps
A howl in the castle walls
Chains rattle in the dungeons

True love's kiss is not his cure

Nothing well wishes can fix
Alone under stone he roars
Until the sun peeks over
And with its dawning light
The prince breathes against stone
Bare skin shivering in the cold
He sheds tears all alone

She came, she kissed, she fled

And now he's left with her curse
Blasted woman of the lunar
Stole away with his soul

If only a kiss

Could transform him
Back to a frog . . .

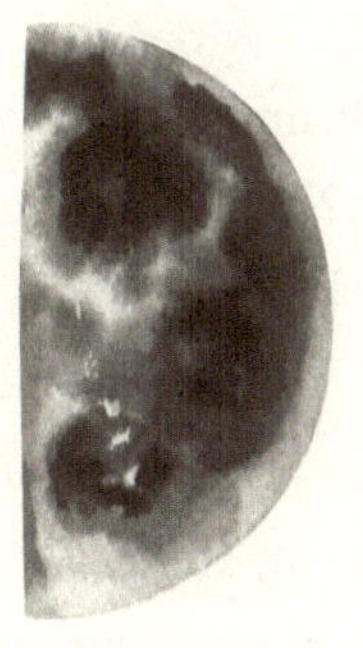

Vindor

Anne J. Hill

Sun slumbers
Moonshifters wake
Doors locked and bolted
Howls drift through southlands
Cover your mouth and hush your heart
Do not fear but listen closely, oh dear child
For the mighty Vindor will slay the beasts tonight

In the Guardhaven Forest, Eliath sat on the log near Haldirth's feet. The five-year-old elf scraped his knife against the stick in his hand, whittling the end to a sharp tip. Through the window, the sun dipped behind the tree line. Though Eliath knew he was safe from the wolves at night as long as he stayed in the town, that knowledge did little to quiet his fears. He *felt* the most secure being close to

Haldirth and his stories of bravery. "Old Man Smithy?" Eliath bit his lip in concentration as his blade snagged on a particularly stubborn knot in his stick.

The silversmith set his hammer down on the anvil. "Yes, child?"

"Tell me a Vindor story?" Eliath moved his eyes from his pointed creation to the gray-haired elf.

Haldirth's brow pinched and he crouched down to Eliath. His voice was a harsh whisper. "Do not speak of such things so freely, boy. Have you told anyone my stories?"

Eliath shook his head, his brown curls bouncing in his eyes. "Not even Tepharē!"

Haldirth gripped Eliath's chin in his hand endearingly. "Well done. Best to not tell your brother any of my tales. Or your mother." He patted the boy's cheek before returning to his anvil. The elf cleared his throat and began. "The legend tells of the Vindor wood elves who lived thousands of years ago. It is said they were bred to be immune to shifter bites, with blood traveling back to the ancients. From the south, they came riding in cloaks of green. Crowns of silver leaves framed their heads and weapons of steel guided their hands."

"Silver like that?" Eliath pointed his knife at the silver charm under Haldirth's hammer.

Using a tong, Haldirth picked up the silver and immersed it back in the fire. "Yes, like this." Flames hugged the metal. "The Vindor emerged from the forest and traveled through southern Nathal, slaying the people who turned into violent animals under the moon. Every night, those bitten by any shifter—moonshifters—contort into their animal skin, lions, wolves, bears, and more. They lose their minds and feast on the flesh of men, elves, and dwarves alike. Like the wolf moonshifters that lurk in our woods."

Eliath swallowed. "I *know* what moonshifters are." He shuddered and glanced at the window. Even though the wolves hadn't stirred yet, their howls haunted him. He knew the guardian would rise soon and all would be well. But there was always a lingering *what if* . . .

Haldirth raised his eyebrow. "Do you want me to tell the story or not, young one?"

The boy swung his leg, tapping his stick against his knee. "Yes."

"Vindor, dawning in the Vindorhaven Forest, were the guardians of the southern lands. Skills like no other, immunity never seen since, and shadows exalting the light."

"Oh! And Vindorhaven Forest is now Guardhaven Forest!" Eliath beamed proudly. "Vindor means hunter—protector."

"Yes." The smith nodded. "But we don't talk about that outside of these walls."

Eliath nodded firmly, his face scrunching in severity. He recited, "We do not discuss the past. We do not discuss war. We do not discuss the outside world. We do not discuss or touch weapons. We are safe. We are loved. We are protected."

Haldirth's eyes were heavy as he nodded. "Indeed . . ."

Eliath's shoulders slumped. "I know the guardian keeps the wolves out of the town, but they're still there every single night. I can hear them . . ." He frowned at the whittled spear in his hand and wondered how useful it would be against a snarling and bloody fanged beast. Guardhaven Forest needed more secret weapons. "Smithy? If the Vindor are gone . . . what happens to us if the guardian dies?"

Haldirth pulled the silver out of the furnace. "You ask good questions. Let me finish my story. As the legend goes, a dwarf, Eyl-Sath, left his home in the Clerthon Mountain Range. He traveled to the south where he met the Vindor. None but elves claimed the Vindor title, but Ely-Sath worked with the best silversmiths, and was able to make an amulet that imitated the Vindor's powers. It took him centuries, but it was done." The silver glowed in the tong's mouth. "From the fire was forged an amulet of protection. When wearing it, Ely-Sath would not turn into a moonshifter. A Vindor made by the hands of mortals."

Eliath stood on the log to get a better look at the metal. A silver wolf head looked back at him, pulsing in red heat. "What made the amulet work, Smithy?"

Haldirth drowned the wolf head in acid and water. It sizzled, and steam climbed up his arm. "That question, my boy, has driven men mad for centuries." He pulled the tongs out of the water and examined his handiwork. A smile slid across his lips. "And I believe I've figured it out."

Eliath's eyes widened. "What's the secret?"

Setting the wolf's head down, Haldirth gestured for Eliath's knife. When the boy handed it over, Haldirth slit his own palm. "Vindor blood." His blood dripped on the metal wolf's face.

Eliath's mouth dropped open. "But Vindor are all dead!"

The blood crackled into the silver. "Indeed. In the sense that no elves hold the same powers. But my great-great-grandfather was among the last Vindor." Haldirth smiled warmly at Eliath. "I have Vindor in my veins. And now this amulet will keep you safe from moonshifters." Haldirth looped a chain through the wolf and draped the necklace around Eliath's neck. The silver was already cool.

The young elf blinked several times. "What?" His spear clattered to the dirt floor. He lifted the amulet and ran his fingers across its soothing edges. "Why for me?"

Haldirth tousled Eliath's hair. He pulled a chain out from under his shirt. On the end hung a silver wolf's head. "I already have my own."

Eliath lost himself in the amulet around Haldirth's neck. A howl pierced the night. The wolves were awakening, but Eliath was no longer afraid.

Eliath will return in Thorn Tower *by Anne J. Hill.*

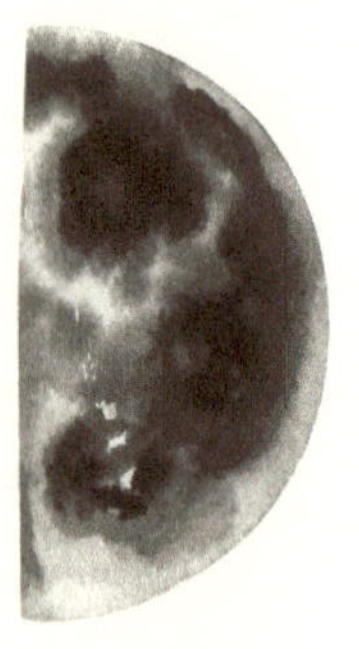

WOLVES AMONG US

MIRIAM WADE

Amidst the halls where learning's light does shine,
A student walks with shadows by her side.
By day a friend to all, so pure and kind;
Yet when the moon ascends, a change inside.
Her eyes ablaze, the beast within unleashed:
A high school werewolf, secreted well.
Her howls resound through midnight's eerie peace,
Conscious of both—her and the lycan spell.
She hides her curse from classmates and from friends,
A double life, she leads with care and guile.
The struggle deep—the moon's pull never ends—
To tame the beast, and all the while, to smile.

Oh, cursed soul, who straddles two extremes,
In twilight's dance, she lives her teenage dreams.

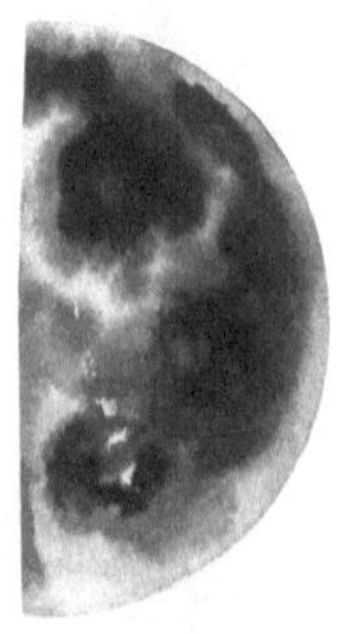

Sunset Skirmish

Hannah Carter

Thirty minutes 'til sunset.

Callum ran a hand down his weary face. He hadn't shaved today—or the last few days—and the long stubble itched.

He glanced out the oval window to the setting sun and sighed. Another night. Another fight. Soon the werewolf transformation would come, and he'd be in misery until the moon set again. He'd come up to the farmhouse attic to attempt a few minutes of sleep, but his mind wouldn't relax—wouldn't stop racing. He'd come to his old home seeking refuge but had yet to find it.

He raked his fingers through his unbrushed brown hair and pinched his eyes shut.

Things had been so much easier when he could drink away his problems.

As he rose, the attic floorboards of his childhood home moaned under his weight. Shredded furniture and chewed knick-knacks littered the ground, and he kicked a fuzzy, wolf-shaped baby toy out of the way. It squeaked with every roll until it landed against a trunk, emitting a last pitiful bleat.

Somewhere on one of the floors below, a door creaked open.

Callum's shoulders tensed, and he gritted his teeth. No one should be visiting a ramshackle farmhouse in the middle of nowhere—not even him, really.

And *no one* should have been opening a door this close to sunset.

He slowly lowered himself down the attic steps. He paused at the bottom, assessing the locked door on his right. Claw marks from last night gouged the wood, but it held firm.

So *it* hadn't opened.

Callum crept down the hallway. He hesitated every few steps, tilting his head to catch another sound.

A large crack broke the silence.

Ah. Someone had stepped on the bad stair.

Callum charged down the rest of the tiny hallway, his fist already reared back by the time he turned the corner. A man in a black trench coat stood at the top of the first-floor stairs, gun loaded.

The intruder's eyes widened right before Callum landed a punch on the man's face.

The stranger staggered back, nearly falling but somehow managed to catch the banister and right himself. His free hand reached for the holster at his hip.

Callum preemptively ducked as the shot fired above his head.

"*Get. Out*," Callum snarled. "We're not bothering anyone here!"

Blood streamed from the man's busted nose, staining his blond mustache and bared teeth. He spat on the staircase and took aim again, but Callum dropped to his knees and lashed out with another blow. His fist connected with the man's stomach, and the bullet exploded the overhead light. Sparks and glass showered both men, and Callum covered his face with his arms—which might have been why he didn't see it coming when the man hammered Callum's head from behind.

Callum tumbled face-first into the glass. He bellowed as the tiny shards tore into his flesh, but he couldn't focus on the pain. He had to move or he'd be shot, right here on the steps.

And how much longer until sunset?

Rolling over, Callum drove his leg into the intruder's knee. The man cried out and fell, and for the first time, he spoke.

"You'll die tonight, wolf. Like the animal you pretend not to be." His voice sounded stuffy and stilted, probably on account of the bloodied nose, but his sneer conveyed more than enough contempt. "But I know who you are. *Murderer. Monster.*"

Callum wiped his mouth, coming away with a dribble of red on the back of his hand.

"You don't know *who* I am," Callum growled.

He lashed out and struck the man's wrist with enough force that a *crunch* sounded. The man yelled, swearing vehemently. Callum snatched the gun up and swung it at the hunter's temple. The blow snapped the man's head sideways and he hit the banister. He collapsed backward, eyes closed, blood spilling down his face.

Callum rose. He winced with every movement, and his forehead pinched together as he swept the bits of broken glass off his arms. The shards crunched underneath his feet while he climbed the stairs.

It couldn't be long until sundown now.

Someone inside the clawed, nearly-destroyed door cried out, "*Daddy!*"

Callum winced, stumbling faster. He wiped his face again, but had no time to wash the blood off. Emeric was used to gore by now, but Callum didn't want the five-year-old to worry.

He barged into Emeric's room. Already, the boy sported wolf ears and a tail, even though a few last orange-and-purple streams of sunlight still lingered.

Callum kicked aside more broken toys and feathers from wrecked pillows and hoisted his son into his arms. "It's okay, Emeric. Everything will be okay."

Emeric's wolf ears drooped. He reached out, tufts of fur sprouting from his fingers. "You're bleeding, Daddy. Something bad happened again—I heard it—"

"I'm sorry. I didn't mean to wake you up. I promise everything's okay." The bed groaned under Callum's weight as he lowered himself down. "Nothing bad can happen when Daddy's here. I promised you that the day you were born." He scratched behind Emeric's ear, which flicked back and forth. "We're gonna stay right here until your mom gets back with the rest of the pack, and then we're going to go live with your grandparents in a place where nobody hunts werewolves. And nobody's afraid of them." He pressed a kiss on Emeric's forehead, but Callum pulled back when fur formed underneath his lips. In a few more seconds, instead of a little boy, he held a wolf cub who wriggled and pawed the air, ready for another night of play.

Sunset.

Callum released his son. Emeric immediately pounced on his new pillow and ripped a mouthful of fabric out of it.

Callum sighed.

He was in for another sleepless night.

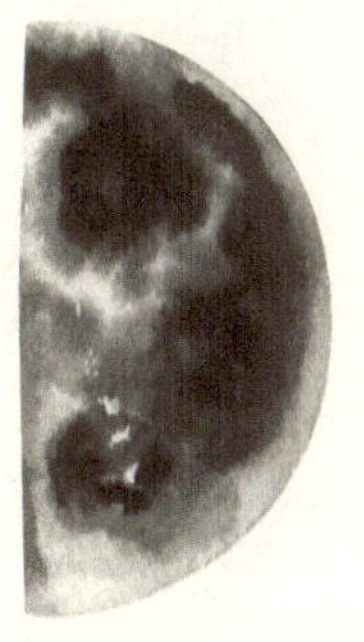

Reshaped

Rachel Lawrence

Once upon a time
I swear, we lived in a fairy tale
Boy meets girl meets idyllic life
And all the happiness we could chase
Together
Memories were magic
For many moons
Nothing could touch us

But darker days brought
Unwanted change
Dreams torn apart

Split right open
And reshaped me into
A mangled monster
In my mirror

You stood by me
As my claws came out
Witnessed all my
Sharpest edges
Resolute in the shadows of
The ways I tried to run
The bite of my scared, snarled words
The fear that trailed me
Like a hunter

You were faithful
As the moon
Shifting with each new season
Consistent
Even in the darkest night
Keeping the tide of despair at bay
Somehow certain
Once the shock had settled
I'd be softer and stronger than ever
In this new skin

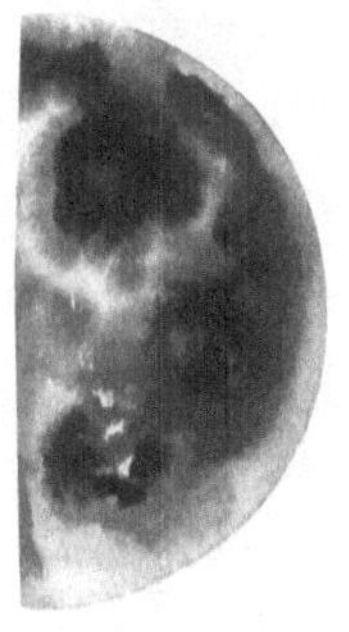

HUNTED

AudraKate Gonzalez

Leaves crunched beneath Verona's feet as she ran through the graveyard and into the woods. The crossbow felt light in her hands; adrenaline coursed through her veins. She was pulled into action when a dark shadow darted out a few yards in front of her. It was fast, but Verona had been training for years. She was more skilled than any of the monsters she'd hunted. After all, a monster's drive was blood and death. No other thoughts ran through their heads. At least no other thoughts that Verona had ever experienced.

"Hey! Wait up!" Tyler shouted somewhere in the distance far behind her. There was no way she'd wait for him to catch up.

Verona had more than just blood and death fueling her. She had something to prove. A need to belong. A duty to her father and the other hunters.

Though female hunters were practically unheard of, Verona's father was a commander in this sector; as his only child, that meant that she was a shoe-in to become a hunter. Something that the other hunters, who'd worked hard to earn their spots, despised. Like Tyler. That jerk had been on her ever since she started training, just waiting for her to slip up.

It wasn't her group's turn to take the full moon shift, but there was a change in the schedule tonight, and Verona was thrilled. Everyone knew that all bets were off during the full moon. Any being could take advantage of the moon's supernatural powers, increasing their own abilities. Zombies could rise. Demons could freely walk. Wraiths could possess. Witches could hex. Wrerds could hunt.

And this Wrerd had thought it could easily sneak past Verona while she was scoping out the graveyard.

She smiled as the wind rushed through her hair and the surrounding woods darkened, her gaze focused on the beast she chased. She lived for the hunt. On her last full moon, she'd staked a vampire who tried to sire a defenseless human. For that kill, she earned her first vampire fang, which Verona had embedded in the hilt of her dagger as a trophy. She couldn't wait to see what her reward for skinning a Wrerd would be. She just had to make sure she reached the Wrerd before the other hunters, before *Tyler*, showed up. They'd turn it into their kill and leave her with nothing to show for.

As excited as she was to be hunting this Wrerd, Verona couldn't help but wish the night to be over so she could spend tomorrow with Lucas. All week he had talked about how he had something really special planned for her. He'd been wanting to tell her something, and Verona felt like her heart would burst in anticipation.

A deadend loomed before them. Coming into view, the ground vanished and dropped off into a ravine. The Wrerd began to slow. It appeared to weigh its only options; either jump—which it *may* survive but then it would have to face whatever creatures were swimming in those waters this full moon—or beg Verona for a quick death. Verona almost laughed when the Wrerd turned toward her. It was going to be her lucky night.

The beast began to shift.

That's interesting. She couldn't wrap her brain around why it would shift when that would only make it more vulnerable. At least in its Wrerd form it had a fighting chance. She sighed, her breath curling in the cold night air, and rolled her eyes. She hated when hunts were too easy.

The Wrerd stood in front of Verona, fur shriveling away to reveal skin, sharp teeth falling to the ground as snarling jowls were replaced with soft lips. Lips that Verona recognized almost instantly. Lips she had kissed all summer.

Verona held her crossbow steady, aiming it directly at his chest. Lucas stretched his palms out toward her. Palms that were just paws moments ago. Her heart pounded, clawing like a beast trying to burst free. *It can't be him.* Lucas was a Wrerd? Her lover. Her best friend. And now her enemy?

Verona's hands began to tremble on the crossbow. They hadn't done that since she was a rookie, a kid. She tightened her grip to steady herself, knuckles blanching. Swallowing a sob, she held a heavy finger over the trigger.

"I thought you said you wouldn't be hunting tonight."

Verona's voice shook. "There was a change in plans."

"Vee, I didn't want to tell you like this," he said, his eyes sad and shoulders drooping.

"You—this whole time?" she croaked. "You've known I'm a hunter! It's my job to kill your kind, and you never said a word!"

"Because I fell in love with you! I was planning on telling you. Tomorrow. Put down the bow, Vee."

She hesitated, her heart weighed down with emotions. He was going to tell her? Tomorrow? Was that why he had been making tomorrow a big deal? But Verona had caught him; he had no choice but to tell her now. And she had no choice but to lower her crossbow to her side with a defeated sigh.

Her brain flashed with thoughts of duty. Thoughts of how she wanted her father to be proud that he'd made the right decision in training her to be a hunter. Thoughts of how she wanted the hunters to take her seriously. What they would do to her if she let Lucas go.

Then she took in Lucas and his chestnut hair sticking straight up. She gazed into those blue eyes that stared at her with longing. With love. He'd never needed her to prove herself to him. In this small bubble they'd built for themselves, she'd felt a sense of belonging. And it was nice to belong to him, with him, even if it was only for a short while.

Duty be damned. She'd face the punishment of banishment for letting Lucas go so he could live.

"Well, well, well, what do we have here?" Tyler stalked toward Verona and Lucas. Verona was so preoccupied with her shock and warring emotions that she hadn't even heard him sneak up on them.

She gripped the crossbow tight and turned, trying to take Tyler's attention off Lucas. "Ty, I've got this handled. You can go tell the others to back off."

"Woah, I don't think so, little huntress." Tyler smirked, unsheathing his sword, causing Verona's blood to boil and her chest to fill with dread all at the same time. "Why don't you leave the big kills to the *real* hunters. Go back to the camp and get some chow started for us."

"*I said I've got this handled,*" Verona ground out, trying to hide the fear that was bubbling inside of her. Fear that Lucas would get hurt. That all of this was going to get wildly out of hand.

But Verona was no actress.

Tyler looked between Lucas and Verona. "Oh my—you and the Wrerd? You have *got* to be kidding me!" He burst out in laughter. Verona winced. "The commander is going to love to hear all about this."

"Tyler, you can't—"

He tsked. "See, this is exactly why women shouldn't get involved in hunting. They always end up with too many feelings. Your father should have known better." As he ran his fingers down his blade, his eyes lit up. "Who knows, maybe when everyone finds out the commander's own daughter was sleeping with the enemy, he'll face his own sort of punishment." Tyler grabbed Verona's chin in his hand, and Lucas growled. "Don't you think Commander Tyler Arlington has a nice ring to it?"

Verona tried to blink tears away, to hide weakness, but it crawled to the surface. "Please," she said, not wanting to beg but she didn't see another way out of this. At least not another way that wouldn't be messy.

Tyler brushed past Verona like she was invisible. He brandished his sword in Lucas' direction. "Don't worry, pup. I'll make this quick."

Schnick!

Tyler staggered forward and slowly turned toward his killer. The arrow from Verona's crossbow protruded from his chest. Blood dribbled from his lips as he stared at her in disbelief. Betrayal. He fell to the ground, a gurgle escaping him as he took his last breath.

The crossbow shook in Verona's hand, but she knew she'd done what she had to.

Lucas took a step closer, looking like he wanted to comfort her. Verona moved away, running to Tyler's side, ripping the arrow out of his body.

How was she going to explain this? They'd know it was her from the wound. She stared at the blood on her hands. It was a crime to betray the hunters. To murder one of them. They'd kill Verona.

As if sensing Verona's fear, Lucas rushed to her, transforming into his Wrerd form. In a frenzy, Lucas tore at Tyler's body. Bones cracking, flesh tearing, he created a canvas of destruction. There would be no way for the hunters to make out that it was Verona's arrow that had taken Tyler's life.

Lucas shifted and wrapped his arms around Verona's waist, kissing her fiercely.

When he released her, she took a deep breath, not wanting to say goodbye, but knowing that was the only thing left to say. "You need to get out of here. The other hunters will be here soon."

"Same goes for you. The pack has picked up your scent." As if on cue, a howl echoed in the distance.

Verona turned her back to Lucas, letting her lip tremble slightly, her hands white-knuckled as she held her crossbow. "I'll have to hunt you eventually. They won't let me live if I don't."

"I know." Silence followed, and when Verona finally gained the courage to turn around, Lucas had disappeared into the gloom of the night, leaving Verona alone amongst the hovering trees. This was all they could ever be to each other.

The hunter and the hunted.

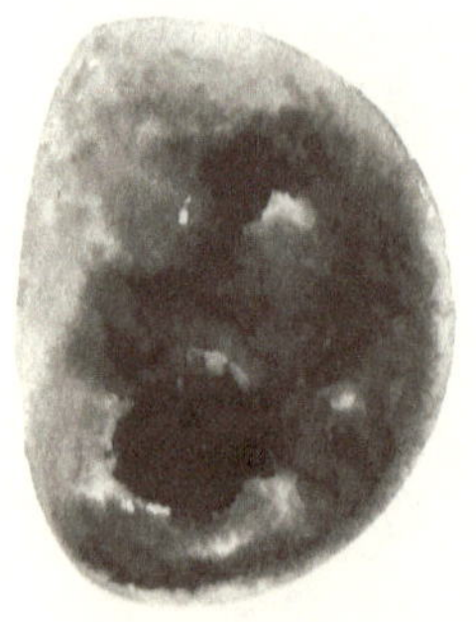

That Man, The Wolf

Elaine Wells

I wonder
where the animal stops,
and the man starts.

He does terrible things
under the light of the moon.
It changes him,
he is uncontrollable,
inconsolable,
a monster of claws and teeth,
helpless to stop the damage he causes.
It is not his fault,

but I wonder
how much human there is left in him,
how much beast there has always been.

I wonder
if the wolf is the reason
or the excuse.

If it is the monster
that commands him to kill,
is it still the man who listens,
is it not his own hand
that does the killing?

He didn't mean to,
but didn't he want to?
Was it the monster that
slaughtered his lover,
tore her to shreds,
ripped the heart from her chest,
or was it the man she is forever explaining,
the one who loves her *almost* always,
except when he doesn't,
but that is not him,
that is the monster.

The man wants the best for her,
the monster wants power,

the monster has a hunger for
brutality,
for cruel savagery,
a gruesome murder,

and I wonder,
if the monster is only
the man uninhibited,
because he wasn't always a beast,
but didn't he always have that anger,
that hatred trapped inside him.

I wonder,
if the wolf is the reason,
or the mask,
the obfuscation,
the dispersion of responsibility?

How could a human have done this?
How could a man be a monster?
But when is it horrible enough
to be inhuman,
Just until it can't be justified.

You have to know
the wolf was always
the metaphor,
'the monster' was just
a moniker,

another name for
the man.

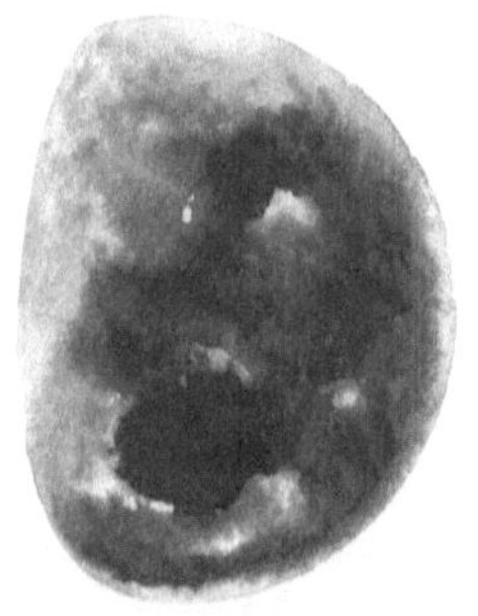

REFORMED

MORGAN J. MANNS

S he's not supposed to awaken yet. It's too soon!"

A frenzy of buzzers and alarms deafens me. Above the mechanical sirens rises a shrill human scream. I can't recall where I am or even *who* I am. Without warning, wildfire flares down my spine, slicing into every vertebra like daggers. *Am I the one screaming?*

A memory resurfaces. I was . . . dying, my body attacking itself. I think I came here for help. But was my inevitable death an accident? A virus? Cancer? I can't remember. I can't think. I can't—

"Secure those straps around her! Tighter!"

Wait, are these people *helping* me?

Shock rocks through me, eclipsing the pain for a blessed moment. That's right. I was bitten. Torn apart and dragged down by a beast. I escaped, and came here for a cure, but every moment with these people feels like I'm slipping one step closer to death.

Voices erupt. I strain to see them, to ask them what is going on. Yet, every time I lift my head, nothing happens. I am trapped within my body. Helpless. It feels as if my bones have become lead—effectively weighing me down.

I blink furiously. Flashes of monochromatic light bombard my blurred vision. I catch a glimpse of hazy figures in white coats rushing around me. Doctors? Desperately, I try to reach for my eyes to tear off the colorless veil. But I still can't move. Leather bands—I realize—hold me down, preventing escape. My fingers claw uselessly against the metal slab under me, finding nothing to grasp. I'm in some sort of hospital room, surrounded by glass walls.

"Her body can't handle this!" a rough male voice shouts.

Blazing heat surges outward from my core, pulsing through every cell. My muscle fibers stretch, and my bones agonizingly reshape. I buck under the restraints as hot tears spill from the corners of my eyes.

Am I going to die?

Their hands hold me still, and the sharp jab of a needle pricks my shoulder as they inject me with more fluids. I thrust furiously. Uncontrollably. There's nothing—

Cool relief floods my arm. My back loosens as I lay blissfully against the table. *They've done it. I'm saved*—It doesn't last. The boiling power within me quickly overtakes the icy sensation, and my blood scorches to new levels. I once again pant and writhe on the table.

"Nothing is working!" another voice cries.

My helplessness turns to wrath. A primal growl edges up my throat as my teeth sharpen into fangs and layer over my lips.

"Everyone, get out of here!" It's the same male voice from before. "Secure the doors!"

The hazy figures hovering over me retreat in a rush. My throat collapses, folding in on itself. *The've given up. Should I?*

I'm slipping farther into darkness, desperately and silently pleading for release. The feeling of suffocation intensifies until finally, it reopens and a desperate howl escapes me.

The wild sound blast slams against the glass-walled room, shattering it into a shimmering rainfall of razor-sharp pieces. They cascade onto the floor, rupturing outward.

Then, just as I think the inferno of heat within me will devour me whole, the pain subsides to a dull ache. My heartbeat thuds in my ears and I feel . . . resigned. Tears evaporate on my cheeks, even as the buzzers still sing the chorus of my destruction.

I flex experimentally and my new muscular body easily powers through the restraints. I raise an eyebrow admiring the ease at which I'm able to move. I breathe deep, then sit up. Someone is in the room with me!

I jolt as I catch sight of the creature that tried to kill me. Turning to flee, the shards of broken glass follow my every movement. The monster mocks me and mirrors my every move. Until—

I peer closer. The monster is—me? My unfamiliar reflection catches in a piece of shattered glass. Nowhere is the slight, comely woman I once was. My body has been transformed into something else entirely. Have I become the very image of the creature that tried to destroy me?

Fur covers every inch of my skin. It's coarse, wiry and blacker than night—blacker than the werewolf that hunted me down. Without pain ricocheting through me I can picture him perfectly—tall, feral and terrifying. As for myself, there's something feminine remaining within my features. I still resemble a human in shape, but my ears are elongated like a wolf's and my eyes are like crescent moons—piercing and glowing.

Something within me has changed as well. There's a lightness there that wasn't present before. An understanding that I was meant to be so much more than what I was.

The people in white cloaks tentatively step from the shadows, back into the broken room. I glance upward, my claws wrapping around the steel table they bound me to. There's five of them—their hands raised in surrendered defense. *We mean no harm*, their expressions say. But can I trust them? What will they do now that they've failed to keep me from becoming the wolf?

I growl and they take a step back, their feet crunching over broken glass.

Within their frightened expressions, clarity finds me.

Coming face-to-face with the beast within, I have a shuddering realization. The glass and I are the same—we have been torn apart and remade into something new and dangerous, all sharp edges and malice.

A smile touches my muzzle as I leap through one of the shattered windows. The exit sign greets me, a crimson beacon in the shadows, as I race into the night. With the moon above as my guide, I run toward a new beginning. Perhaps the werewolf who bit me was not leading me to death, but to a life worth living.

There's only one way to find out.

I howl, seeking the one who transformed me. I am reformed—granted another chance at life.

It's time I used it for something greater than myself.

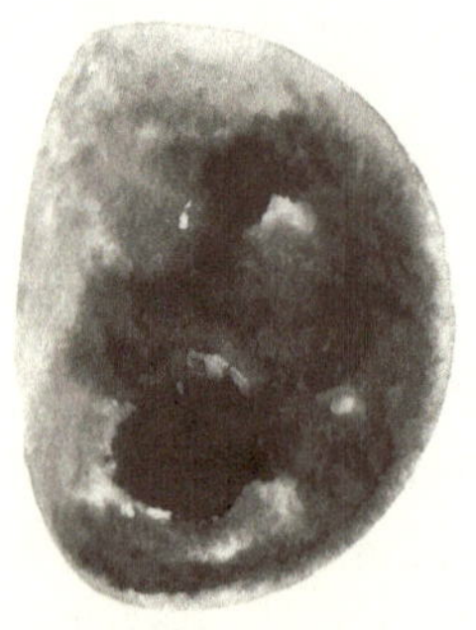

Cursed Moon

Miriam Wade

Oh, wretched moon that hangs above my head,
Thou art the bane of my accursèd plight,
For every month thou fill'st me with dread,
And robb'st me of my sanity and might.

I loathe thy cold and unforgiving gaze,
That pierces through my very soul and skin,
Turns me into a beast for nights and days,
A creature that doth revel in its sin.

Thou art the curse that I can never break,
Constant reminder of my savage side,

And though I strive to keep myself awake,
Thou dost compel me to give in and hide.

Oh moon, thy beauty is but a cruel lie,
For thou hast made me what I most despise.

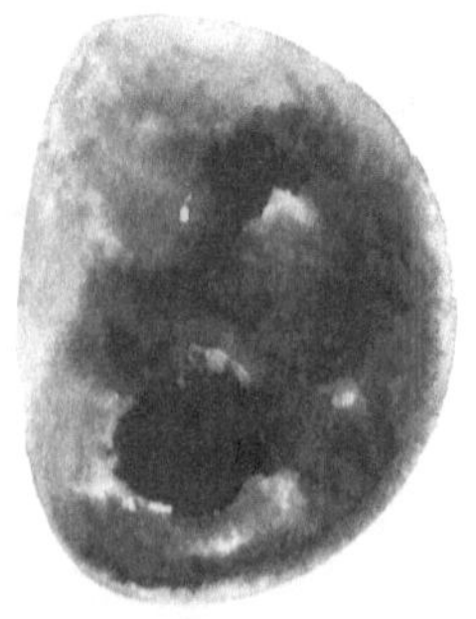

RIPPED

AudraKate Gonzalez

*T*he case of Jack the Ripper is one of the most famous unsolved mysteries of England. Jack the Ripper was an unidentified serial killer who hunted the streets of Whitechapel, London in 1888. He killed five women, and possibly several other victims, in manners that led constables to believe he had knowledge of human anatomy. What many will not tell you about are the hairs found on the bodies. Hairs that could never be matched to any person. Hairs that would show that a Canis Lupus had been in close contact with the victims. A coincidence?

Whitechapel, London—1888

The band played loudly in the public house. Everyone whooped and hollered to the music as trumpets and cornets, piano and violin, vocalists and clapping hands joined together in uplifting harmony. It was night, and the gas lamps were dimmed, adding to the warm ambiance of the room. There was a cacophony all around the pub, sounds of excitement and joy.

Yet Alice only felt melancholy. Her senses were dulled from the pint of alcohol she held in her hands as she stood next to the bar. She was careful not to spill a drop. Alice knew she should put the glass down; her body wasn't cut out for the strong drink, but she needed to forget everything.

It was Alice's fifth night in Whitechapel. She was visiting her cousin, Anne Marie, for a few weeks to get over her failed relationship.

Alice had been engaged to the esteemed Lord Victor Palmer, youngest son of a duke, but it had fallen apart after she caught Victor with another woman. Alice was furious, crushed, confused. She had thought both her relationship and her wedding plans were perfect . . . but it turned out Victor was only marrying Alice for appearance's sake and her family's societal prominence. The girl Victor truly wanted was low-born—not someone his family would ever have approved. He'd called Alice a prude for how she'd reacted to the whole situation. A name that's haunted Alice ever since.

Her father was furious at her when he'd learned about the broken engagement. He blamed everyone but Victor, even going as far as firing Alice's governess, claiming she'd failed to shape Alice into the perfect wife. He could barely look at Alice, which made it unsurprising that he'd agreed to her visiting Anne Marie. He probably assumed that if Alice ended up a spinster, she'd at least know how to work in charity.

The whole scenario made her feel as though she was a rope being pulled in two different directions; her father wanted her to be the epitome of high society and Victor truly wanted a woman that was carefree.

Alice twisted the ring she still wore on her finger. Victor had told her to keep it in case she had a change of heart and agreed to his mistress. She had plans to pawn the thing, but for now she liked the way it looked on her finger. Her hand seemed naked without it, though it felt oddly weighty with the dead dreams of the future it once held.

Anne Marie had invited her to Whitechapel. She'd been residing in Whitechapel for a few months to help with the less fortunate. It was honest work that Alice knew her cousin really enjoyed.

Anne Marie was focused on being a caregiver, and her family was very approving of that, for now at least. She had no suitors, no status to uphold. She was free to live her own adventures and enjoy Whitechapel, thanks to the charitable work she was doing there. She spent her days in Whitechapel with those in need, and at night she would unwind by dancing.

Alice watched as her cousin moved amongst the other dancers; she was fluid, appearing comfortable in how closely they were danc-ing. Touching men's hands without gloves between them. Picking partners with no dance cards in sight.

Alice felt even more out of place than she usually did at dances. She felt stiff and cold like a porcelain doll.

Alice hoped she could learn from Anne Marie. Unfortunately, despite all the events they'd already attended together, Alice still couldn't free herself. A sense of propriety ingrained in her by her father would not allow it.

Whitechapel was vastly different from the streets of Windsor, where Alice lived with her parents. Whitechapel was wild, a division of London that seemed to live by its own rules. There was excessive drinking and partying every night. There were no dance cards adorning wrists or perfect treats that chefs spent days preparing. Propriety was a fleeting thought. Women earned their own money. It was hard labor, mostly in laundry or factory settings, and not exactly the type of work Alice was looking for, but she was fascinated by the independence of Whitechapel women.

Not everything about Whitechapel was ideal. The living conditions were poor, with dozens of people crowded into every building, and there had been talk in the newspaper about a murderer running rampant. Someone stalking the ladies of the night and killing them in terrible ways. They called him "Jack the Ripper."

Alice shuddered. It wasn't safe to wander the streets alone at night in Whitechapel. Then again, it wasn't safe anywhere at night.

A woman's laughter drew her from her thoughts. The sight of her cousin's blonde hair bouncing throughout the dance, free and wild, had Alice raising her hands to ensure her own hair was properly pressed in place by a multitude of pins. The idea of her hair spilling around her as freely as her skirts made Alice nervous.

The man her cousin danced with murmured something in her ear, and Anne Marie giggled.

Alice wasn't brave enough to join the crowd of revelers. There were too many people out there. Too many men she didn't want touching her. She wondered if Victor would be surprised to see her in a place like this, at night, with no chaperone. Would he be impressed? Would it make him want her? *Only* her?

What would her father think? Would he completely disown her if he knew her whereabouts?

There were very few who knew of Anne Marie's lifestyle. She'd always kept conversation around what she did everyday vague. Of course, everyone in their family knew about her work with the poor, but the rest of what she did with her time? That was information reserved only for those closest to Anne Marie.

Alice shook her head free of thoughts about her father. This was her time to prove to herself that she didn't have to follow the rules laid out for her by men.

Alice, gripping her cup tightly, crept a little closer to the dancers, her steps slightly shaky from the alcohol.

A man bumped her shoulder; her drink splashed over the rim of its glass onto her green dress. Startled, and somewhat annoyed, Alice set her glass down and swiped at the spot with some napkins she found on the counter.

"I'm so sorry about that, miss." The man stared at her with strange, golden eyes. A shade she had never seen so bright before. His beard was trimmed short, giving him a rugged but distinguished appearance. The dark, working-class suit he wore made it easy for him to blend in with the crowd. Alice couldn't even remember if she had spotted him before this encounter. His smile was nice, inviting, but also oddly unnerving. With a jolt, she realized that despite the light in his eyes, they seemed completely devoid of life.

Alice narrowed her own eyes. She was tempted to wave the old engagement ring around to ward him off. The ring was beautiful, pure silver with a delicate diamond protruding proudly from the center. She was surprised the man hadn't already seen it from across the room.

Instead of replying to his apology, Alice returned to wiping the stain away, making sure the ring would catch what little light there was.

"Are you all right?" He grabbed Alice's elbow. Now in his close proximity, she breathed in a terrible, stomach-souring scent that reminded her of a wet dog left out all night in sewage.

Alice took a large step back from him, though with his hold on her arm, she could not get away. His eyes flashed—not with anger, but intrigue. A piece of her dark hair had slipped from its bun. Releasing her elbow, the stranger swiftly tucked the strand behind her ear. She stumbled back further.

Oddly, he sniffed the air around her, and again he reminded her of a dog. "Had too much to drink, have we?"

Alice didn't respond.

"You're not much of a talker, are you?" The man gave a slight grin.

She wasn't used to men coming on this strongly, but maybe it was just how they were in Whitechapel. "I'm as chatty as a church bell. Too much so sometimes, my cousin tells me," Alice lied.

"Well then, maybe you'd like to tell me your name?"

She blotted the stain. "I'm Alice." The alcohol had a hold of her words, and her name was out of her mouth before she could stop herself.

"Alice."

The way her name rolled off the man's tongue caused her skin to crawl. A small command inside of her begged her not to continue the conversation, and when Alice made out that the voice was her own and not her father's or Victor's, she listened.

Alice put her prickly guard back up. "I'm not in the mood to talk to a strange man in a pub who clumsily spills drinks on ladies.

Especially not when my fiancé is right over there." She hoped he wouldn't hear the tremor in her voice as she pointed off in a random direction. Her finger landed on a man stumbling around to the music.

The stranger looked where she'd pointed and smirked as if not fooled at all. "This is the wrong place to come to if you aren't going to talk to strange men." He took the used napkins from her hand, brushing her fingers as he did. She watched him eye the ring and quickly pull his hand away as if she'd burned him. Was that disdain that crossed his face?

"Why would someone let a beautiful lady like you stand here all alone?" He raised an eyebrow.

"I'm not alone."

"*Of course* you aren't." Sarcasm dripped from his voice.

Alice crossed her arms defiantly. "I can go wherever I want to without a chaperone."

The man scoffed. "Not in this town."

Alice's cheeks grew hot. She had met her fair share of entitled men in her twenty-four years, but this one had definitely taken the biscuit on how he thought he could speak to a woman and touch her without asking. It was downright rude.

"So, your fiancé brought you here to this seedy pub instead of staying at home? May I ask where home is?"

"Win—" She stopped herself. She'd had enough fun and adventure this evening. It was time for her to leave. She steeled herself and stared right into his eerie golden eyes. "Excuse me, sir." Alice shouldered past him and made her way through the crowd.

"Where are you going?" he called after her.

She whipped around. "Far away from the likes of you. It doesn't matter whether a lady has come to a pub or attended a party alone or with friends. We have every right to decide who we will or will not talk to."

The man grinned wickedly, running his tongue across his pointy canines.

Alice's stomach churned at the sight. *What a louse.* She turned around and didn't glance behind to see if he followed, but she felt those unnerving eyes boring into her.

Pushing through person after person, interrupting dance after dance, Alice finally made it to the center of the room. Anne Marie had partnered with a different man now and was completely engrossed in the dance, her eyes filled with alcohol as she spun around her partner.

Alice tugged on Anne Marie's yellow sleeve. Her cousin twirled into her and smiled at Alice. "Allie! Isn't this amazing? Such a party!" Alice could barely hear Anne Marie over the band and people around them. "Oh, I'm so rude! Allie, this is . . ." Anne Marie turned to the man, squinting as she tried to remember his name. "My apologies, I don't know if I caught your name." The man seemed to neither hear Anne Marie nor notice Alice. He was lost in the dance. Actually, judging by the smell seeping from the sweat encircling his shirt, he was lost in the drink.

Alice scrunched her nose at the scent. "I think it's time to go home."

Anne Marie shook her head as though she hadn't quite caught what Alice had said.

"I want to *go.*"

Anne Marie pushed her dance partner away and pulled Alice to a more secluded corner of the room. Apparently, Anne Marie's partner wasn't all that attached to her, as he quickly moved on to another girl he'd found in the crowd.

"Allie, if we leave the pub now, before closing time, we'll look like such prudes!" Anne Marie protested.

Alice winced at that word. *Prude.* That was exactly what Victor called her the last time they'd spoken.

Not wanting to be accused of cold rigidity again, Alice nodded in understanding. She didn't want her cousin's reputation, whatever that reputation, to be ruined. If Anne Marie didn't want to seem a prude, then so be it, but Alice wasn't going to stay a moment longer. She couldn't wait to be back in the safety of Anne Marie's flat. Seeing that man, and remembering the way he'd touched her, his entitlement, made her flush with anger.

"Well, I'm going to the flat. Try not to be out too late. There's a strange man here . . ." Alice turned to scan the crowd, wanting to point the man out to Anne Marie, but he was nowhere to be found.

Her cousin rolled her eyes as she drifted back to the crowd. "Allie, there's a lot of strange men here. Stay safe, cousin! I'll see you at home." And with that, Anne Marie's willowy figure was swallowed up by the dancing bodies once again.

Being used to the lit streets of Windsor, Alice was taken aback by the blanket of black that covered Whitechapel. This was the latest she and Anne Marie had stayed out. The streets were eerily quiet, like the silence of catacombs. It wasn't exactly empty, Alice realized. She held back a scream as a rat scurried across the street in front of her. Tempted to run back into the pub, she clenched her fists and kept on.

Darkness followed Alice as she went, occasionally broken up by the full moon peeking through the crouched structures surrounding her. The labyrinth of crumbling dwellings seemed much more sinister in the midnight hour. The sound of her heels on the cobblestones comforted her. Solo footsteps meant that she was alone, and that was all right with her.

Somewhere ahead, water dripped into an open sewer drain. The smell of refuse tainted the air. Alice covered her nose, passing by an alleyway dotted with strange shadows. Her chest tightened at the sight, and her skin tingled. *Was something in the darkness watching her?* Entranced by the sensation the alley gave her, Alice couldn't seem to move her feet.

One shadow separated from the others, looking too large to be a man but too strange to be a mere animal. It stood on hunched legs and seemed to face her. Its broad shoulders filled the alley, and a growl rumbled down the dark tunnel. Alice's lungs tightened as her breathing came in short, quick gasps, claustrophobia squeezing her. The shadow moved from the blackness and lurched toward the moonlight. Alice's breath hitched as the figure stalked closer.

"Oi, sorry miss." A constable bumped into Alice's shoulder, surprising her and pulling her out of her trance.

Were her eyes just playing tricks on her?

"Dark out 'ere, init?"

Alice timidly nodded. "Sure is." Dryness had settled in her mouth, choking her words. She slowly turned back to the alley. Everything looked normal. No shadows. Just inky black darkness heavy with the smell of sewage.

"You alrigh'?" the constable asked.

Alice gave him a smile, even though she knew it would be hard to make out her gesture in the dark. "I'm well. Thank you, sir."

Something crashed in the distance, grabbing the constable's attention. "Well, be careful walkin' 'round out 'ere." The constable dashed toward the noise, and Alice continued in what she thought was the direction of the flat. She turned various corners and down different pathways. It wasn't until she reached a dead end that she realized she must have gotten turned around somewhere.

Heavy breathing that was not her own sent Alice into a rigid state. This was the wrong place to get lost in the dark. Her feet slowly moved in the direction of the panting. When she turned around, two glowing lanterns hung suspended in the air.

No.

They were golden eyes.

The man from the pub stared at her, his clothes now torn and hair disheveled. A sinister grin spread across his face when he took a step closer. He stopped in a beam of moonlight and looked up. He inhaled the night air deeply, and then there was a loud *crack* as his body contorted in a horrifying way.

The man was bent over, bones protruding from his suit while he shifted. Fur sprouted in places that used to be skin. Claws shot out where his fingernails once were. Alice was frozen in her spot, her legs quivering at the beast the moon illuminated before her.

Its brown, matted fur had a sweaty sheen in the light. Its ears were perked high on its head, as if he found excitement in hearing Alice's heart hammer in her chest. Tattered clothes—strands of a white shirt and very torn pants—still clung to its thick, muscular body. Alice's eyes traveled back to the beast's face as she forced herself to stare at what she could only describe as a werewolf from a penny dreadful.

The werewolf shifted its gaze to Alice, clearly on the hunt by the way its mouth salivated. Its eyes glowed with a fierce hunger and its nostrils flared, taking in her scent as if committing it to memory. It prowled toward her with terrific grace. Sweat trickled down her neck and trailed down her bodice.

As the air around them turned hot with tension, a familiar smell arose in the alley. A smell that Alice would never forget. A wet dog left in the sewage.

Fear traveled through her, engulfing every thought, every function, turning her insides into a dark abyss as hollow as a doll's body.

Teeth bared and claws extended, the wolf lunged forward. It reached for her neck, and its claws grazed her throat. Alice dove away from the beast, crashing into the wall of the building that blocked her path. Pain lanced across Alice's neck; she grasped at her throat, trying to staunch the hot liquid that flowed from the wound.

The werewolf sniffed the air and inhaled deeply; he must have caught the smell of her spilled blood. She finally found her senses and screamed, a choked, blood-curdling cry. It shattered her eardrums, but that seemed to be as far as it went.

Fur bristling, the werewolf snorted at Alice as though thrilled at her failed attempt.

The sound raised her own hackles. This was not the way Alice wanted to die—alone in an unfamiliar alley, killed by some monster. But if she did die, she wanted to do it fighting against her murderer.

Alice scrambled to her feet, heart pounding in her chest as she faced the monster, daring it to fight her. The werewolf swiftly pounced on top of Alice, knocking her back to the ground. The air whooshed from her lungs, leaving her breathless as stars exploded in her vision like a celestial fireworks display. Her head connected with the cobblestones in a sickening *crack*. A whimper slipped out of Alice that sounded much like a kicked puppy. The throbbing in her head sent her adrenaline pulsing even more. She summoned her strength and reached up toward the beast's face. She yanked her hand away, bringing a fistful of the creature's fur along with it. The monster snapped its teeth, narrowly missing her cheek. Alice seized the moment, delivering a powerful blow as she smashed her elbow against its face.

The wolf howled, its nose twitching from the hit, which gave Alice enough time to scramble out from beneath it. She was too slow. The beast dragged a sharp claw down her side, digging into her flesh and pulling her back beneath it.

Their battle raged on, a morbid symphony of clashing wills and primal instincts. Alice thrashed like a possessed warrior, fighting the wolf from her position on the ground in ways she had never seen. In this moment, there was no such thing as rules. Propriety didn't exist here. It wasn't about who her father or Victor wanted her to be. This was about survival. She would no longer worry about failing anyone. Alice would live whatever short moments of life she had left for herself.

The odds were stacked against her; the monster didn't even act like it could feel her blows. In fact, it was most likely *letting* her fight back. The blood loss from her wounds, mixed with the black spots now peppering her vision, was making the battle seem impossible.

The werewolf's maw was inching closer to Alice's already torn neck, and Alice was ready to give one last blow. The silver of her diamond ring caught the light of the moon. Alice jabbed her whole fist directly into its right eye. She made sure to gouge her ring in as deeply as she possibly could, twisting and turning it while blood oozed down her hand. There was a *pop* and then a *sizzle* as the ring dug in. The smell of burning flesh permeated the air. Her finger felt hot as the silver burned into the wolf.

Alice channeled all of her hurt and anger into her hand. She was tired of men ruining her life. Tired of how they thought they could do whatever they wanted to a woman with no consequences. Break her heart. Lie to her. Touch her. Control her. *Kill* her. Alice would be a victim to men no longer.

A howl ripped from the beast's throat, piercing the night. It pulled its face away from Alice, snarling.

Alice fell limp, her strength and adrenaline completely depleted. Only one golden eye glared down at her now. Maybe she wouldn't win, but at least she could tell the reaper that she died trying. It brought a smile to her lips to know that the wolf's eye—the man's golden eye—was something it would never get back.

The werewolf took his sharp claw and sliced into her abdomen with precision, but she was numb to the pain. Alice wanted to close her eyes; her world was starting to fade as she felt liquid ooze around her body, her diamond ring now ruby and charred. Then the werewolf stopped, ears perked in the air as it listened. Alice felt vibrations rumble through the cobblestones beneath her. Footsteps.

With one last growl and a glare in Alice's direction, the monster took off into the darkness.

A bell rang from somewhere around her. Then a hand reached down and touched her wrist, pressing firmly as though searching for a pulse.

"We got a live one o'er 'ere!" a man shouted.

Survivor on Church Street—1898

When the woman known as Alice Acker was found alive, having survived the attack, many were hopeful that she would lead authorities to the capture of Jack the Ripper. Unfortunately, due to her severe wounds, Alice lost the ability to speak, and any of her writings on the subject were too incoherent to be believed. The only conclusion that could be drawn was that she was not in fact a victim of The Ripper and instead a victim of some other horrible tragedy that left her with a terrible case of trauma. No one knows what became of Alice Acker—or Jack the Ripper—after that, although it is believed that he somehow found passage to America, where he lives out the rest of his days . . . perhaps even continuing his nefarious deeds.

New York City—Present Day

The club was hopping. Sweat and glitter covered the floor as bodies ground against each other to the beat of the music. The DJ was blasting a raucous mix that vibrated the drinks at the bar.

A man hovered near the counter, cradling his drink close to his chest as he watched the spectacle in front of him. It was like the club goers had lost all control of their bodies.

Fools. All of them.

He noticed a girl standing alone in a corner. She seemed out of place, pressed against the wall, gaze darting in every direction. It was never a good idea for a girl to be alone. There was always someone on the prowl. Someone like him. And he'd make sure that she didn't get away. He never lets them get away nowadays, especially after the one girl.

She hadn't been meant to survive, yet somehow, she'd bested him. Took his eye— and his pride—with her. It'd taken him quite a few years before he gained the confidence to kill again. And by that time, he was far away from the streets of Whitechapel.

Like he'd done so many times before, he bumped into this girl's arm, spilling her drink down the front of her shirt. "Oh, I am so sorry, miss."

She looked up at him, her stare stopping on the patch covering his right eye. "Oh, it's totally okay. I don't like this shirt much anyway." She laughed nervously.

The man laughed too, making sure to reveal his charming smile.

She held out her hand to him. "I'm Melanie."

He shook it. "Jack." He winked. "Hey, you wanna get some fresh air? This music is starting to give me a headache."

Melanie glanced toward a group of people—her friends, he assumed—who were completely lost in their dance. They wouldn't even know she was gone. "Sure, I could use some fresh air."

Jack held his arm out to Melanie, and she linked hers through it before he led her through the crowd.

Outside, cars and people buzzed along the street, but Jack kept Melanie in the dark confines of the alley. His favorite setting for a kill.

The fresh air felt great, and the moonlight glittered all around him. His body started to ripple beneath his clothes as he thought about shifting.

Then a sound at the end of the alley caught his attention.

Melanie pulled herself closer to his side. "Jack, what was that?" Her voice shook.

He moved closer to the dead end of the alley. A figure separated itself from the shadows, stepping into the moonlight. A woman stood before them with torn clothes, wild hair . . . and a giant scar across her throat.

"Hello, *Jack*." Her voice came out harshly, as though it pained her to speak.

He didn't need to ask who she was. He'd assumed she'd died long ago, but it appeared as though his curse had rubbed off. A thought that had never crossed his mind before. "Alice," he sneered and began to shift.

Melanie screamed and took off down the alley toward the streets. Jack growled, but he couldn't pursue in the middle of a shift. He'd take his anger out on Alice for ruining his late-night snack.

"Lovely night for a full moon," Alice said in her gravelly tone, and then she transformed as well. In that moment, as Jack stared at the vengeful gleam in Alice's eyes, he knew that she was just as determined to finish this once and for all.

Shapeshifter

Morgan J. Manns

son of nightfall,
embrace shadow's form.
transform under moonlight,
become reborn.

sharp claws and fangs
within you, emerge.
with the forest as your ally,
let wild power surge.

look past insatiable hunger,
allow your heart's fire to burn.

don't let the world hold you back;
you're ready to unlearn.

what brought you here
was not simply a bite.
it purified the darkness,
allowing you to fight.

to battle against foes
more deadly than you,
they'll try to undo
what made you anew.

join with the pack,
and get ready to prowl.
because coming together
you surely will howl

do not be afraid
under the moon's watchful glow.
those thorns in the night
only help blood flow.

remember, son of the night,
you've been released with a purpose.
become the shapeshifter,
and scratch more than the surface.

THE ADMIRER

BROOKE J. KATZ

Crackling blazes light up the night, bringing the forest to life as smoke and sparks slip through the few remaining leaves in the great oak trees. Distorted rap music thunders from the boombox that rests on an open tailgate. Lucky has a love/hate relationship with these gatherings. They used to be more fulfilling, but he's found that he has lost his sense of satisfaction by the end of the night. He wonders what the point is anymore. The dark cloud over Lucky has been following him around for at least two years; he just can't shake it.

The stench of sickly sweet perfume chokes his senses and the cheap beer these college students consume makes him want to gag. It definitely doesn't help the burning sensation in the back of his throat. Lucky clenches his fists. How much longer should he wait? The throbbing behind his left eye sends shooting pain through his sinuses. He pinches the bridge of his nose, rubbing his fingers down the sides, but the pressure doesn't lessen with the massage.

He sighs. Even at twenty-two, he feels ages older than these college kids. Their laughter rings through his ears. Couples dancing off to the side are silhouetted by the fire in the middle of the clearing. A group of five—what he assumes are frat boys, based on the matching Alpha Phi hoodies—slam beer cans to their foreheads while playfully shoving and hollering at each other like a pack of wolves. Lucky rolls his eyes and cracks his neck. They do not have a care in the world. The little idiots are clueless as to how one night can change your life. That's why he loves these gatherings: the unaware mortals, their dulled senses. He surveys the area, counting roughly twenty party-goers and only two vehicles.

"Sorry, bro!" One of the drunk frat boys crashes into his chest. Lucky pushes him off.

"No problem, *bro*," Lucky returns, mocking through gritted teeth. Lucky jerks both his exposed white t-shirt and flannel collar back into place.

Lucky's body quivers, and he tastes blood. Quickly, he wipes his lips. He needs to calm his emotions; letting anger control him is sloppy.

The frat boy meets Lucky's eyes, and his Adam's apple bobs as he swallows. The boy backs away, all humor vanished from his face.

Lucky breathes in, counting to ten. Crisp leaves swirl around him, and branches creak as the wind sweeps through the glade, kicking up a familiar scent. Apparently, he isn't the only kindred spirit out here. Uncrossing his black-jeaned legs, he leans against the truck behind him. His spine tingles; his muscles grow taut. Lucky scans the area for the source of the scent, only to find that the couple seated across the fire from him are making out like nobody's around.

"Disgusting," he mutters, averting his gaze to continue his search.

"No kidding, like get a room." The truck dips and groans. Lucky glances over for the source. His chest expands. Apparently, he didn't have to search hard.

"Want a water?" Her voice is lyrical and her legs swing energetically from the tailgate. He takes the water bottle from her tan, slender hand. Her skin is smooth and her nails are as sharp as thorns.

"Can I help you?" he asks gruffly. What could this woman want? His bones ache as the hunger grows.

Her eyes glint with golden flecks similar to his own irises. She doesn't flinch or pale like the others but meets his gaze evenly.

"Thanks." He eyes her suspiciously, but curiosity wins. He cracks the bottle open, trying to quench the burning sensation in his throat.

"You looked hungry . . . I mean, *thirsty.*" She shows off her canines.

Lucky arches an eyebrow at her mischievous smile. His eyes trail down to her pink lips and beyond, following the jagged scar on her slender neck. Her cropped tie-dyed sweater exposes her smooth stomach, and cut-off shorts show off her legs. She's petite. Thick, curly brown locks are tucked behind her ears. She looks sweet, he won't deny.

"I hate these parties." She crosses her arms. Lucky shifts his feet crossing one over the other, her attention diverts.

"Hey, nice kicks." She playfully nudges his leg with the tip of her high-top Vans, which are the same as his. Who is she? He recognizes her, but from where? She taps her thigh with her pointed red nails.

"Why are you here if you hate it?" He rolls his neck and shoulders before taking another swig of water. His skin is on fire and the girl's gaze is unsettling. Her smile holds a secret.

"Same reason you're here tonight, Lucky."

His eyes snap to hers; he recognizes the look. It's the same one he sees in the mirror . . . Mercilessness.

"Who are you, and how did you know my name?" he growls.

"Easy there, Tiger. Call me an admirer . . . Or Sasha . . . Whatever strikes your fancy." Her nails have morphed from sharp, delicate thorns to thick, pointed weapons. "I just had to meet the infamous Lucky who leaves a trail of blood wherever he goes; the loner with no pack to answer to."

"Yet here you are, intruding on my dinner time. Who are you, really?"

"That was how long ago now?" Sasha taps her chin, eyes narrowing.

"Answer the question." Lucky's voice deepens as his dilated pupils stare into her own golden irises.

"You really don't recognize me, do you?"

He searches her from head to toe. The only thing he recognizes about her is her scent. His nostrils flare, inhaling her deeply. Fresh earth and rain.

"Think back, Lucky. We heard about you, the boy who went insane and killed his pack. The warning about you went down the chain once you killed the alpha of the next pack and his members. You were a loose cannon, a psychopath that no one could stop. You left no survivors— until one night, a year ago, you messed up." She rubs the scar on her neck. Then Lucky remembers: her wide eyes, her sweet scent. He keeps his breathing even. She can't see how leaving her alive has unnerved him. His boredom has made him sloppy.

"I found your scent at a gathering like this one a month ago." She scoots closer to Lucky. "I stayed back and have been following you at a distance ever since. Learning from you, growing in the same hunger and thirst as you. My alpha. I will do anything for you." She brushes his knuckles with her fingertips. He crosses his arms.

The little she-wolf looks at him, her eyes not filled with fear but admiration.

"I think I understand you," Sasha continues. "No one respected me either, Lucky. You did me a favor that night. I was forgotten in that pack, pushed aside and abused. You set me free. Is that why you do it? Did your pack abuse you too? I've always wondered why you work alone." Her "sweet girl" act is good, but her heart rate and the hunger in her eyes indicate a different story. The hatred for what was done to her runs deep. She wants revenge.

"What if I told you I just hate people and there is no reason except the joy of draining the life from someone?" Lucky smirks at her, but she doesn't waver.

"Maybe that's so, and I get it. I've had fun learning from you." She tilts her head, her hair falling over her shoulder. "Though you're not as thorough as you thought you were. I've had to finish off a few for you. We could make a great team." She crosses one arm over her abdomen, resting her elbow on it as she brings her nails to eye level, examining them.

To spice things up a bit, he murmurs, "I'll tell you a secret I've never told anyone." He leans in, his nose touching the hair tucked behind her ear. She shivers—but is it in pleasure or in fear? It doesn't matter. "I was a beta, and I caught the alpha of my pack with my girlfriend. I don't trust people. I work solo." He catches a whiff of her intoxicating scent and struggles not to lose control. He presses back against the taillight of the pickup.

"That doesn't explain why you killed everyone and continued on alone with your murder spree." She challenges him, chin lifting. He considers playing around to see what she is capable of. Until now, she has been the shadow lurking in the background. Why not let her shine and entertain him a bit? This could be amusing.

"Maybe I'll tell you after dinner. I'm famished, aren't you?" Lucky licks his lips and his fangs protract.

"Very." Her own incisors protrude. "Together?" She looks at him expectantly.

"Ladies first. Show me what you've gleaned from me." He waves a hand arm towards their audience. He relaxes against the truck, crossing his arms and waiting for a show.

Sasha hops off the tailgate; turning toward him, she does a little curtsey. He likes her spunk. Her body cracks and bends at odd angles as she transforms into the most gorgeous wolf he has ever seen. Her fur appears soft to the touch, and its milk chocolate color looks sweet enough to eat.

She hunches, the fur on her back standing on end. Her incisors sparkle in the firelight.

"Dude, that girl just turned into a wolf!" someone shouts. It doesn't take long for the screaming and madness to follow.

Sasha goes first for the bro who fell into Lucky. She doesn't kill him right away; she rips a chunk of his wrist off so his hand dangles limply from his arm. His blood curdling scream echoes through the party. He is soon silenced with a bite to the neck; the she-wolf shakes him lifeless.

Lucky raises an eyebrow. She's quick, but not as skilled as him. Her kills are more sloppy. Lucky would have gone around the circle; she seems to go after those who annoy her the most.

Sasha moves to the next meal, the making-out couple who had been sitting across from them. The guy took off screaming the moment the she-wolf attacked the first frat boy; but the girl sits there paralyzed, wide-eyed with terror and open for the taking. Sasha tears her limb from limb, not even giving the girl a chance to scream. The she-wolf licks the blood from her snout and rounds on the guy, who hasn't gotten very far. He screams for help before she lunges for the back of his neck.

The two pick-up owners realize they don't have the keys they foolishly left in their sun visors. Little do they know the keys are just under their trucks. The music continues playing, giving this massacre a soundtrack. Lucky watches with amusement as the humans scramble and trip over their own feet and each other. The incoherent screaming and shouting satisfies him. He chuckles. Blood pulses through his veins, the hunger strong he can taste the blood.

Lucky can see the pure joy in her monstrous grin as she goes from one meal to the next. His own monster comes alive as she devours each one. She rips throats open, going for the heart last. Blood splatters his face. He swipes his finger across his cheek and licks it clean. He inhales the salty scent of her carnage, his eyes closing in ecstasy. His little admirer pants hard after her show. Her bloody fangs drip with plasma, the iron tang inviting Lucky in.

Her panting turns to a growl as she circles back to him. Her fur stands on end. She isn't finished yet.

"Impressive, little admirer, but it looks like you left one more victim for me."

She looks over her shoulder towards the forest. Her golden eyes dart around as if she's counting to make sure. Stupid little wolf.

Others may find the transformation from man to wolf uncomfortable, but not Lucky. He can finally stretch and crack his weary bones.

It's *his* time to play.

Sasha's eyes snap back to him. There is fear in them for the first time tonight. Her thoughts connect with his, her desperation seeping through the words.

There are others of our kind that want to stop you. You need me, Lucky.

He bares his teeth. *Foolish little wolf. You should be careful who you admire because you could be admiring the devil.*

He doesn't bother with the limbs; he goes straight for her throat.

Sasha is just as sweet as he remembers her.

He leaves just a touch of life in her. Her breathing is shallow and ragged as he stalks over to the hearts she left behind, sucking the life from them before double-checking the crowd.

Sasha did teach him something tonight. Make certain that your plate is clean and that you finished every last bite. Satisfied there are no survivors, he returns to Sasha. The invigoratingly crisp air hits his naked skin as he transforms back into human form. He squats down before the she-wolf and traces the scar through her fur. The same one that he left a year ago.

"I never answered your question, Sasha. After that first kill and the power I felt, I knew I never wanted to share that again. I don't want to be tamed or have a pack hold me back from my hunger." Lucky wipes his mouth. "Thank you for the show. You made dinner rather easy tonight." He stands, stretching his arms to the moon. "My little admirer, thank you for awakening me."

He shifts back into a wolf, releasing a satisfied howl before sinking his teeth into her throat.

Beneath A Moon So Pale

AudraKate Gonzalez

Gather 'round and listen
To a deadly tale.
So gruesome does it grow
Beneath a moon so pale.

The monster is reborn
With fur as dark as sin
And claws as sharp as thorns.
The hunt can now begin.

The wind moves through the trees
Your scent caught on their boughs.

Demons track with ease.
There's nowhere to run now.

Teeth as sharp as blades
Trapped nightmare's gore.
With no one to be saved,
The beast will haunt forevermore.

Beware its cursed bite,
This creature of the Devil.
Its howls pierce the night.
In your blood it will revel.

Gather 'round and listen
To a deadly tale.
The wolf is coming for your soul
Beneath a moon so pale.

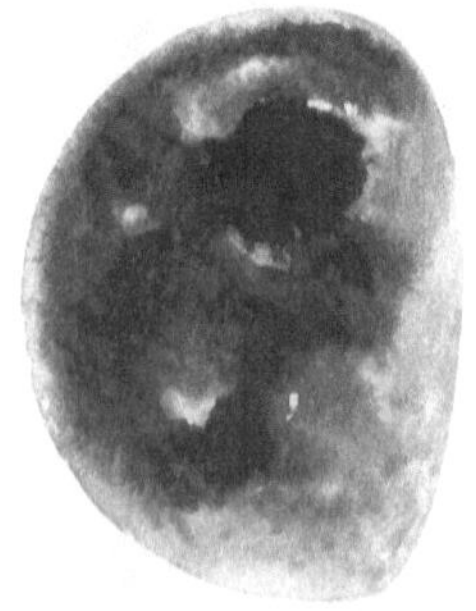

THICKER THAN BLOOD

MARY AGNES RATELLE

The tall buildings and even taller trees of Joliet loomed over-head and a cold wind pierced through me as I stepped across the pavement. I hadn't set foot in Joliet since I had moved to Chicago all those years ago, but still, the familiar streets of my old hometown stretched before me and tugged at my heart like a noose around a prisoner's neck. I clutched a bouquet of flowers wrapped in newspaper close to my chest, the blue pigments of the irises bleeding into the edges of the paper and blurring the date at the top—January 29th, 1921. Soon, I approached a stone gateway. The words "Oakwood Cemetery" were carved on one of the posts with deep, clean strokes. I walked past rows of gray headstones until I came to a small grave that sat beneath a great maple tree. The bare branches quivered in the wind and shook glittering specks of snow to the ground. I gazed at the inscription.

Alice O'Mally

Born April 23rd, 1896

Died February 5th, 1903

I bowed my head, pulling my scarf closer around my ears and chin. Tears flooded my eyes and soaked into the material as I thought of my childhood friend, a wave of memories overcoming me.

The river.

The blood-stained ice.

The shallow grave beneath the snow.

Each memory unfolded like a switchblade and cut through my chest. I fell to my knees as more tears filled my eyes. I reached into my pocket for my handkerchief and my hand brushed over the folds of an envelope.

Violet's letter.

I didn't need to look at the letter to remember what it said. I had only received it two days ago, but the words were already branded on my mind.

Dearest Edith,

I know you haven't forgotten about me. Prison bars can never keep me from you when blood binds us together.

Come visit me. I have some tantalizing news to tell you.

Ever yours,

Violet

My heart winched as I brooded over my sister.

Violet was ten years older than Alice and I, but she preferred playing with us rather than with girls her own age. In the summer we played chicken on the nearby train tracks and in the winter, we slid on the ice of the Des Plaines River, testing how close we could get to the thinnest patches without falling through. Whenever the ice cracked beneath our feet, Violet would roar with laughter and encourage us to slide farther out. Violet made us promise not to tell anyone about our games, and Alice and I dared not breathe a word. We could never refuse Violet anything. Back then, I thought nothing of our games or of Violet's strange habits: her nightly walks, the claw marks outside her window, the coarse tufts of animal fur I would find in her clothing.

I hardly understood the curse then, but how I wish I did.

My heart sank into my chest at the realization, like a smoldering coal left to die in a cold hearth. I looked at the little headstone again. I unsheathed the flowers from their newspaper wrapping and gently placed them on the grave, glancing at the newspaper as I folded it. A bold headline at the top of the page read, "The Moonlight Slasher of Chicago Takes Another Child Victim."

I shuddered. *Violet would be fond of him.*

I wadded the paper into a ball and buried it deep in my pocket. The wind circled around me once again, surrounding me with frost and biting whispers.

As the sun faded in the sky, I trudged up the street toward Joliet Women's Prison. The towers flanking the front entrance cast long, dark shadows upon the limestone of the massive building. I stepped up to the front entrance and a prison guard led me down a long hallway of cramped cells, stopping at a cell toward the end of the hall.

Before the guard had the chance to say anything, a woman's voice like crisp satin cut through the silence. "Edith, you've come."

I squared my shoulders and stood firmly in front of the cell. "Only because you sent for me. I'm not here for my amusement."

"You have fifteen minutes," the guard said before disappearing down the hallway.

I nodded and turned my attention back to the prison cell. It was dark with dim shards of light emanating from the small window in the right corner. Violet sat on the floor in the opposite corner, her knees tucked up to her chest and her arms lying limply beside her. She chuckled softly. "After seventeen years, my little sister is finally visiting me in prison. You've grown so much since I last saw you!"

"You said you have something to tell me," I replied. "What is it?"

"Not so fast. I want to hear about the outside world," Violet murmured. Her voice was smooth and soft, like the purr of a cat. "I hear that there's a killer in Chicago. Is that right?"

"Yes, is he a friend of yours?" I retorted.

Violet laughed. "Oh, if only he was. He and I could have filled Oakwood Cemetery with dozens of little graves."

My face grew hot. "You're disgusting," I snapped.

Violet inched across the floor until a thin beam of light fell on the right side of her face. Her exposed eye glinted in the orange light as the corner of her mouth curled into a smile.

"I miss it," she said coolly. "The planning. The chase. The feeling of victory when the deed was done. If only I weren't trapped here and I could go on the hunt one more time."

My stomach turned and I pounded my fist on the wall beside the cell door. "That's enough. I don't want to hear this."

"You'll understand the feeling one day."

I froze. "What do you mean?"

Violet slipped back into the dim light. She slid onto her stomach and crawled low across the floor on all fours, her gaunt hips and shoulder blades making strange shapes in the shadows as she moved. She approached the bars and stopped a finger's length away. She let out a long, labored breath. "I'm dying, Edith."

Shock pricked the inside of my chest like needles in a pin cushion. "What?"

"I'm dying. For seventeen long years I've been stuck in this prison, starving for the taste of something warm. Something *fresh*. It's caught up with me now. I don't have long."

"Good," I said coldly. "Then the curse will die with you. The world will be better off."

"Oh, Edith." Violet smirked, leaning closer to the bars. "How little you understand."

My blood fumed like hot tar within my veins. "I understand perfectly. The curse, the condition—whatever you want to call it—is passed down from mother to eldest daughter. Grandmother passed it to Mother, and when Mother died, she passed it to you. You have no children, no eldest daughter to inherit it, so the curse will die with you."

"But there's the caveat," Violet said. "Since I have no daughter to inherit the curse, it will go to my next of kin—*you*."

My heart beat in my chest with a rapid, unsteady rhythm, the sound filling my ears until I could scarcely hear myself speak. "You're wrong!" I said through gritted teeth.

"But I'm not wrong," Violet replied. "The curse *has* to live on, and it *will* live on through you."

"It won't. It *won't*!" I countered, fighting back angry tears.

"Oh, but it will," she said, nearly laughing. "You'll be just like me, little sister."

"A beast, you mean? A wolf?"

"Yes, a sometimes-wolf," Violet mused, rolling her head back to rest against the wall beside her. "You'll be a woman who can slip into the world of beasts, and a wolf who can masquerade as a human."

"But you always wanted to be a wolf—to be just like mother," I stammered. "No matter what I become, I'll never be like you."

"You say that now," Violet whispered. "But you'll think differently once it happens. One day you'll feel it . . . the *Hunger*."

"The Hunger?"

Violet pounced upon the bars, which rattled against her weight as she grasped them with her long, skeletal fingers. I staggered backward, nearly tripping on the stone beneath my feet.

"The *Hunger*," Violet growled through her bared teeth. "A hunger like none you've ever known, one that cuts through your stomach and into your soul. A hunger that will only be satisfied with blood and bone."

I felt cold to the pit of my stomach. The blood drained from my face and I wanted to faint, but my last spark of resolve kept me on my feet. I couldn't grovel to Violet, even though I feared in my heart that she was right.

"But don't I have a choice?" I said at last. "I may become a wolf, but can't I choose whether or not I become a beast?"

"Nature will always surpass choice," Violet said. "Such is the world of beasts."

I crossed my arms, pulling my coat tightly around me. "I'll never be a beast," I replied, the spark inside me growing stronger. "Even if it kills me."

A door opened at the end of the hallway, and the guard's heavy footsteps echoed off the walls as he tread toward me. Violet pressed her face close to the bars.

"But don't you see?" she said in a biting whisper. "You already have a little beast within you. We both know that I couldn't have made my first kill without you."

Violet's words curled around me like a chain.

"Time's up," the guard said.

I nodded and followed him without uttering another word. As I walked away, I heard Violet call out to me one last time. "Who knows," she called. "Maybe that killer in Chicago will have a rival."

I returned home to Chicago that night and a week later, I received a letter. A sick feeling twisted in my gut as I read "Joliet Women's Prison" scrawled on the front flap of the envelope. After staring at it for a moment, trembling, I took a breath and tore open the letter.

Violet was dead.

A prison mate had sent the letter, detailing how Violet had collapsed in the prison yard only two days after my visit. My whole body went numb as I read the letter and stuffed it in my coat pocket. I turned the news over and over in my head as I went to work that morning, the hustle and bustle of the busy streets of Chicago barely penetrating my consciousness. Soon, I approached a brick school building that overlooked the streets of Armour Square. I stepped through the front entrance and plodded down the hallway to my classroom.

I closed the door behind me and sat down at my desk, surveying the items I'd left there. A stack of first grade readers sat next to my two good fountain pens and my battered copy of *A Child's Garden of Verses* by Robert Louis Stevenson. Absently, I placed the letter on top of the poetry book, my mind too cloudy to consider hiding in between its pages.

Someone knocked at the door, jolting me out of my trance. "Come in," I called.

Mr. Carney's balding head poked through the door. "Miss Granger," he said in a low voice. "Did you hear the news?"

"What news?" I asked.

A woman—Miss Blake—peeked over Mr. Carney's shoulder. "About the Moonlight Slasher!" she interjected. "His last victim was from Armour Square—a student from James Ward!"

My heart sank. "I didn't hear that part. Our students are already terrified enough as it is."

Mr. Carney removed his glasses. His eyes were red and shiny. "I tried to get Principal Ferris to discuss it at the school assembly, but she thought that would only scare the students more. I don't know what we can do to help them."

"What we should do is figure out who this killer is," Miss Blake said.

"And how are we supposed to do that, Miss Blake?" Mr. Carney countered.

Miss Blake ran her fingers down the Marcel wave that framed her face. "Look for clues and give our findings to the police," she replied. "We have to use our imaginations."

"As much as I would like to catch this killer," I said, "I think the only thing we really can do is look after the children."

"My only point is that it doesn't hurt to be observant," Miss Blake insisted, glancing at my desk. "Like so . . ."

She picked up the envelope on my desk and withdrew the letter. "Joliet Women's Prison . . ." she read, glancing at the return address. "Edith, what's—"

"That's private!" I exclaimed, snatching the letter from her hand.

Miss Blake winced as the edge of the paper sliced across her palm. A scarlet thread of blood oozed from the cut and ran down her fingers.

"Oh goodness, I'm so sorry!" I said.

"Maybe now you'll think twice before being so observant," Mr. Carney said, trying to hold back a hearty laugh.

"Why do you have a letter from Joliet Women's Prison?" Miss Blake prodded, ignoring Mr. Carney.

"Family matters," I replied stiffly. "It's private."

I took out my handkerchief and pressed it against Miss Blake's hand. The scent of blood filled my nose. My mouth began to water, and my teeth itched at the thought of the taste. Horror shot through me; I ripped my hands away, gagging.

Miss Blake looked at me quizzically. "Are you all right?"

"Y-yes," I stammered. "It's just . . . the blood."

"I didn't think you had such a weak stomach," she scoffed.

I let out a polite chuckle and wrapped the handkerchief around her hand. At that moment, the clock chimed the half hour. Miss Blake muttered, "Thank you," and made her way to the door. Mr. Carney followed her, only to turn back to me for a moment. "Are you sure you're all right?"

I nodded. "Fine."

A sympathetic smile flashed across Mr. Carney's face, then he turned to leave. I was alone again. My stomach gurgled eagerly. *I'm just hungry,* I told myself. *That's why I reacted the way I did. It's nothing more than that.*

My stomach gurgled again, as if in disbelief.

The day crawled on, my insides feeling stranger with each hour. My stomach churned inside me, as if it was trying to break free from the rest of my body. I distracted myself with work, but the memory of all that had happened was mere steps away from my mind. Morning turned to afternoon, and I stood in front of my desk, looking out at the little faces that stared back at me from their seats.

"Who remembers the name of our poem from last week?" I asked.

A hand shot up. "'My Shadow'!" a girl with dark brown pigtails blurted out.

"Wait until I call on you, Lucia," I replied. "But you're correct, it was 'My Shadow' by Robert Louis Stevenson. Who can recite the first stanza for me?"

Lucia and two other children raised their hands. I called on a girl named Maria. Out of the corner of my eye, I noticed two boys in the back row whispering to each other. One boy was drawing something in his composition book, and the other was looking over his shoulder.

"Jack and Francis," I called. "Please pay attention while others are reciting."

Francis shot me a sheepish glance and put his pencil down. Jack sat still in his seat, but his eyes were still glued to Francis' drawing.

"All right, Maria," I said. "You can begin."

Maria stood next to her desk and began:

I have a little shadow that goes in and out with me,

The whispering in the back continued.

And what can be the use of him is more than I can see.

Lucia, who sat in front of Francis, turned around in her seat and joined in the boys' discussion.

He is very, very like me from the heels up to his head;

Jack whispered something, and Lucia's face turned white.

And I see him jump before me, when I jump into my bed.

Jack said something else and Lucia began to cry. She fell back into her seat, hiding her face behind two balled up fists.

"My goodness, what's going on here?" I exclaimed.

Maria stopped and turned to look at the back rows. The other children twisted in their seats and stared curiously at the commotion.

"Nothing," Jack said, shrugging. "We were just looking at Francis' drawing."

"And what drawing is that?" I asked, making my way to the back row.

Francis quickly closed his composition book. "Nothing."

"It certainly doesn't sound like nothing."

Francis blushed all the way to his forehead. He picked at the edge of the cover of his book for a moment, then opened it to the incriminating page, which showed a drawing of a tall man with a long black coat. He walked down a winding street, following a child who seemed unaware of the stranger's presence.

"It's the Moonlight Slasher! See?" Jack exclaimed. "Francis saw him."

"No I didn't," Francis stammered. "Stop saying that!"

Lucia continued to cry, and I put my hand on her shoulder. The other children fidgeted around in their seats and chattered to each other.

"But you said you did," Jack insisted.

Francis hid his face behind his composition book. "No, I didn't! My brother just told me about him."

"He takes people away," Lucia sobbed. "I don't want to be taken away!"

"No, he *slashes* them," Jack said, making a dramatic slashing motion with his hand. "He slashes them with a big knife. That's why he's called the Moonlight *Slasher*."

"Stop it!" Lucia buried her face in the crook of her arm.

A few children began to weep while others pushed through the crowd, eager to see Francis' drawing. The commotion swirled around me like a swarm of bees. I picked Lucia up and went to the front of the classroom, balancing the child on my hip as I managed to clap my hands three times. "Boys and girls, return to your seats!"

Some children immediately sat down, but a cluster of them gathered around Jack, peppering him with questions.

"Is the Moonlight Slasher big and tall?"

"Where does he hide his knife?"

"Does he only come out at night?"

I clapped my hands again. "All of you in the back, return to your seats."

Reluctantly, the remaining crowd did as they were told, their attention still transfixed on the gruesome stories that Jack was all too eager to supply.

"Boys and girls," I said, "I know this news is frightening, but I assure you that you're all safe here."

"But Jack said that the Moonlight Slasher could slash through the door," Maria exclaimed.

"It's impossible to cut through a door with a knife," I said. "Jack's just telling you a story."

Lucia looked up at me, a shred of hope in her teary eyes. "You mean the Moonlight Slasher is just a story?"

I was silent. My heart ached, ripping in two as I beheld the trusting faces that stared up at me from their desks. I hugged the little girl tightly for a moment.

"No, he isn't just a story," I began. "But you're safe here. Nothing will hurt you, and I'll do everything I can to keep you safe."

My heart ached again. My words were such a hollow comfort. My stomach twisted and gurgled inside me, draining the blood from my limbs and making me cold to the touch.

The school day finally ended, and I went home. My apartment greeted me with weary arms and the quickly setting sun cast dark shadows against the two chairs that stood on either side of the empty kitchen table. I slumped myself at the table and buried my face in my hands. Hours passed, and I didn't move. Grief hung over me like a fog, blurring every thought until each was indistinguishable from the other. In the silence, a pang of hunger echoed from the pit of my stomach.

Slowly, I got up and made my way to the kitchen. I grabbed a loaf of day-old bread from the breadbox and devoured it, slathering each bite with butter. I finished the loaf, but my stomach still raged with hunger. I went to the pantry and withdrew a bag of soft apples and another bag of potatoes, then, sitting down on the floor, I gobbled down the apples, cores and all. I dug into the potatoes next, their milk smearing across my face with every bite of the crisp, raw potatoes. Each morsel echoed in my stomach like a pebble dropped into an empty cavern. My body began to shake. I tried to stand up, but weakness overtook me. Instead, I crawled across the floor on my hands and knees as I searched the kitchen for more food. Hunger consumed my every thought, and I wanted nothing more than to satisfy the growing emptiness inside me.

Nothing filled it.

I found some cold chicken in the icebox and I ripped my teeth into it. My stomach growled inside me like a beast desperate to be set free. It demanded more. It demanded something meatier, fresher.

Bloodier.

I gulped. Long, pointed nails sprouted through the ends of my fingertips. Coarse brown hair spread down my arms and across the backs of my hands. I cried out, but the only sound that came from my lips was a piercing howl. I burst through the door and rushed into the empty street, nearly colliding with a group of stockyard workers returning home. They exclaimed in Italian to each other, and I tore down a nearby alley. I ran as fast as I could, barely detecting the ground beneath my feet. I could only think of running, my mind laced with thick fog. The sound of the wind blowing over the tops of the buildings and the shrieks of passersby became fainter. I cried out again, the sound ripping through my throat like broken glass, and before I knew it, the whole world went black.

In a place between consciousness and unconsciousness, I saw her again.

Alice.

She was walking through the brush along the bank of the Des Plaines River. Her face was shining in the late afternoon light, and her eyes were bright and eager. "Is the ice patch Violet wants to show us much further, Edith?" she asked.

"It's not much further," I heard my voice reply. "Violet said that it's so thick, you can walk to the other side of the river."

Alice grinned. "Violet always finds the most exciting things."

We walked farther into the brush until we found Violet waiting for us beside the river. "You found me!" she exclaimed, jumping to her feet. "I have to show you the ice. It's so clear that you can see the fish swimming beneath it."

Alice jumped onto the ice, excited to follow Violet's lead. I was about to step on the ice myself when Violet stopped me. "No, no," she said. "The ice is only thick enough for two people to walk across it. I'll show Alice first."

"All right, I'll wait here then," I replied.

"No, you have to go back into the forest and keep watch for us. No one else can know about this patch of ice," Violet said. "If too many people come, they'll scare away the fish."

I nodded. Without another word, I walked back the way I came. About halfway through the forest, I decided I had gone far enough and sat down beside a tree to wait. After a moment, I heard a scream— a sharp, agonizing scream that cut through the dense wall of trees. I leapt to my feet and ran toward the riverbank.

All I saw was blood.

Hideous blood.

And Violet's monstrous figure standing over a little lifeless body.

I awoke to darkness. Only a thin ribbon of light emanated from the crescent moon and lit my surroundings ever so slightly. I felt the biting cold of the snow packed around my body as I lay limp on the frozen ground. Tears flooded my eyes, and I wiped them away with the back of my hand. Wiry hair brushed past my eyes, and a sudden dread overcame me.

Slowly, I sat up and examined my form. My long, mangled limbs cast monstrous shadows on the snow as I moved them about, and a deformed snout jutted from my face, my tongue detecting a set of sharp teeth. Everything came over me in a wave, and I cried out into the darkness. The cry turned into a scream—a scream as piercing as a steel blade, a scream of complete horror and disgust. I screamed until I no longer could and fell back on the snow, exhausted.

A strange smell wafted through the air and reached my nose, which twitched in interest. I turned my head to see a wide creek only a few feet away, the water fuming and bubbling as it released the potent smell. I was near Bubbly Creek. The waters fed on the waste from the nearby meat-packing factories, devouring each morsel and bubbling with vile satisfaction. I was sickened by this, yet my stomach gurgled eagerly as I continued to sniff the air. I gritted my teeth and continued to study the bank. A row of trees stood before me; their trunks covered in claw marks. My heart in my throat, I searched the snow for any signs of violence—for traces of animal fur or blood—but I found nothing. Tentative relief creeped into my heart. The trees were my only victims.

Shakily, I got to my feet. I walked downstream from the creek, following my tracks back to the street. I crept on all fours and slunk through the shadows, hoping that none of the drunks or policemen that inhabited the streets at this time would see me. As the night turned into day, my human form slowly reemerged. I hurriedly covered my nakedness with the rags left from my dress and ran through the streets until I reached my apartment, thankful that the blue veil of the early morning covered me.

After filling a basin with hot water, I scrubbed away the grime that still clung to my skin. Then I quickly dressed and pinned my wild hair back into a low chignon. I was hungry for breakfast, but I was too afraid to eat anything. Instead, I cleaned up the mess I left in the kitchen from the night before and left for school.

A crowd of policemen, parents, and children had gathered in the front hallway of the building by the time I arrived. A group of parents surrounded Principal Ferris, sobbing and waving their arms in a panic as they all spoke at once. A few policemen weaved through the group and took Principal Ferris aside. I spotted Mr. Carney standing near the far wall.

"Mr. Carney," I called, pushing through the crowd. "What happened? It isn't . . . It can't be . . ."

Mr. Carney nodded slowly, his eyes red and tear-stained. "Yes, it's happened to us."

My blood grew cold. "Who . . . Who . . ."

Mr. Carney put his hand on my shoulder. "It's Francis. He never came home from school."

I could scarcely breathe. "So, he's missing. He could be all right; we just need to find him."

"No," Mr. Carney said gently. "He's dead. His parents received a letter this morning with one of his coat buttons inside. It was from the Moonlight Slasher."

A sob like a lead ball filled my throat and expanded with every breath I took. "I promised him. I promised all of them that nothing would happen."

"Miss Edith Granger," someone behind me said.

I turned to find two policemen. One was well beyond middle age, with a thick gray mustache, while the other was younger. "I'm Inspector Hawk, and this is Officer Grant," the older one said. "Principal Ferris told us that you were Francis Callahan's teacher. Could we ask you some questions?"

"Yes, of course," I replied.

I took a moment to gather myself, and then I followed the policemen into an adjacent classroom. Officer Grant withdrew a notebook and looked at Inspector Hawk expectantly.

"Miss Granger," Inspector Hawk began. "When did you last see Francis?"

My stomach twisted into knots, but I forced my voice to be steady. "Yesterday at three o'clock, which is when I dismissed class for the day."

"And what did you do after that?"

"I went straight home."

"Did you leave your home at any point after that?"

"I did . . ." I faltered. "I went for a walk that evening, around eight o'clock."

"And what time did you return home?"

I fingered a lock of hair that had come loose from my chignon. "I'm not entirely sure," I replied, choosing my words carefully. "But I went to sleep at about a quarter to nine."

Officer Grant glanced up from his notes. "One of the other people we questioned this morning mentioned that your sister had been charged with murder some years ago. Is that true?"

I twisted the lock of hair around my finger more tightly. Anxiety grazed the inside of my stomach like the tip of a sharp knife, cutting deeper and deeper as it moved toward my chest.

"Yes, that's true," I continued after a moment. "But that happened a long time ago."

"Would you describe your relationship with your sister as close?" Inspector Hawk asked.

"No, I rarely spoke to her after she was arrested."

"When was the last time you spoke to her?"

My chest tightened, as if each question was squeezing out every breath I had left in my lungs. "Last week. She . . . she's dead now. She knew she was dying, and she wanted to speak to me before she died."

"What did you talk about?"

The strands of hair snapped between my fingers. "Family matters. "Do you have any more questions?"

"No," Inspector Hawk said. "You're free to go. Thank you, Miss Granger."

I slipped out of the room, but I lingered for a moment by the half-closed door.

"I hope I wasn't out of line asking that question," Officer Grant whispered.

"No," Inspector Hawk replied. "You were right to ask that. It doesn't prove that Edith Granger did it, but it does put her under some suspicion. Violence often runs in families."

I felt sick. A pang of guilt overcame me, and I ran out of the building and into the schoolyard. I leaned against the brick wall of the school as I gasped for air.

A few children were running around the yard, taking advantage of the chaos inside for a few extra moments of play. I saw Jack among them, only he wasn't playing. He paced along the perimeter of the schoolyard, his arms folded tightly and his eyes cast downward. I walked over to him. "Are you all right, Jack?"

Jack nodded his head furiously, tears shining in his eyes.

"It's all right to cry, Jack," I murmured.

"I was supposed to walk home with Francis," Jack said through uneven sobs. "But I didn't. Miss Blake asked him to stay behind to help her with something, and I didn't want to wait for him. It's all my fault."

I fought back tears as I listened to Jack, my heart like shattered stone. I hugged him. "You're only a child. You're only a *child*."

Jack didn't respond. Instead, he howled, a shadow of grief and confusion swallowing him whole.

The days dragged on, the cloud of death hanging over them. With each morning, reports of wolf sightings grew more frequent, and some theorized that the wolf and the Moonlight Slasher were one and the same. Although the police maintained that the murderer was almost certainly human, "wolf" quickly became synonymous with "killer," and the pain of my transformation overwhelmed my being.

I passed the short mornings and the interminable nights like a corpse—cold and distant. Pitiless hunger echoed through my being and shook my very bones. I tried everything to curb it, but no amount of food could satisfy it. Some nights nothing but my sheer will kept me in my human form, and other nights I was overcome by the hideous form of a wolf.

On those nights, my whole body ached and mourned like it had never mourned before. My voice pierced the air with a howl so pitiful that it felt as if the entire world grieved beside me. I deserved the contempt of the world, the rejection of nature itself. I was neither human nor animal.

I was a shadow.

A shadow inside of a shadow, hollow and afraid.

One of these long evenings, I stayed at school later than usual. I couldn't go to my apartment, for I feared that the beast would overtake my weak body once I was alone. I paced up and down the dark hallways, clenching my fists together and taking slow, labored breaths. When I was tired of the hallway outside my classroom, I went upstairs. The door of the domestic science classroom was ajar, letting a little light into the otherwise dark hallway. Voices emanated from the room. One was unmistakably Miss Blake's, but the other sounded much younger. I crept up to the door to listen for a moment.

It was Lucia's voice.

Why is she here so late? I thought.

I listened again.

"Lucia, could you hand me that box of ribbon?" Miss Blake asked. "I just need to finish the quilt display for the domestic science handicraft show, and we'll be done for today."

"Yes, Miss Blake," Lucia said. "Will we be done before dark?"

"My goodness, it is getting dark, isn't it?" Miss Blake said, her tone bright. "Do you have anyone to walk you home?"

"No, Papa is working at the stockyards tonight," Lucia replied.

"What about your mother?"

"Mama died when I was born."

"Oh, that is a shame," Miss Blake said, an odd note in her voice. "So you don't have anybody?"

"No," Lucia said.

"Would you like me to walk you home? I don't want you out there alone, particularly with everything that's happened."

Lucia agreed to Miss Blake's offer. Something about this arrangement struck me as strange, as if it were calculated. I slipped into the broom closet and watched them disappear down the hallway, slinking after them as soon as they were too far away to hear my footsteps. Hiding in the shadows, I followed them as they trudged through the snow-covered streets. At first, Lucia directed Miss Blake where to go, but soon Miss Blake took over. "No," she would say. "It would be much faster if we went this way."

Lucia shivered, but she obeyed Miss Blake's directions. My limbs twinged as I walked towards them, the beast trying to emerge from my body. I gritted my teeth, hoping that I could hold my transformation off for a little longer. The sky became darker and darker, and soon we arrived at a secluded street near a line of trees. A horrid smell filled my nose; we were nearing Bubbly Creek.

"Where are we?" Lucia asked.

"Before I take you home, I have to show you this place." Miss Blake grinned. "Follow me. It's through these trees."

"But it's dark," Lucia whimpered, peering through the trees with a sheepish eye.

Miss Blake reached her hand out to Lucia. "Don't worry, I'll be right here."

Lucia took Miss Blake's hand and followed her. With her free hand, Miss Blake pulled something out from under her coat. My heart pounding in my chest, I tore down the street, through the trees and down to the riverbank. When I caught up with them, I could scarcely believe the sight before me. The edge of a blade glinted in the moonlight—and Miss Blake was holding it over the cowering child.

"Don't you harm her!" I growled, urgency permeating my every word.

Lucia screamed. Miss Blake reeled around, nearly dropping the knife as she did so. "Who's there?"

I stepped out of the shadows, determination crackling through my chest like lightning. "Stay away from her!"

For a moment, Miss Blake squinted into the darkness. "Miss Granger," she said at last. "What are you doing here?"

"I followed you," I replied. "I know what you're up to."

"Up to?" Miss Blake grabbed Lucia by the arm.

Lucia squirmed, distressed tears flooding her eyes.

"Don't play innocent," I snarled. "I know who you are."

All at once, Miss Blake's kindly demeanor disappeared. She stood tall and foreboding, like the bare trees that towered over us. "Yes, but who else would know?" In that instant she lunged at me, knife in hand.

I leapt to the side, but my foot caught on a tree root and I collapsed to the ground. Miss Blake grabbed my wrist and wrenched my arm behind my back. I tried to wriggle free, but her grip was too tight. She hunched over me and grazed the edge of the knife against my throat. "And between the two of us," Miss Blake whispered in my ear, "who already has a killer in her bloodline?"

The fire in my veins smoldered as hopelessness overcame me. I closed my eyes and I felt the beast clawing at my insides, begging to be free. Or perhaps, this time, *I* was the one begging, as if I were reaching for a strength that was always inside me. From the corner of my eye, I noticed Lucia cowering behind a nearby log. My heart swelled with pity for the child; I couldn't let Miss Blake take her life too. My shoulders dropped as I relaxed every tense muscle in my body and for the first time, the wolf and I shook hands.

In that moment, the beast emerged from my fragile human bones. I ripped my teeth into Miss Blake's arm. She screamed but still held fast to the knife. I threw her off me, but Miss Blake sprang to her feet, brandishing her knife and standing agape as I transformed before her eyes. I pounced upon her and pinned her to the ground before flicking a glance at Lucia. She was inching her way across the riverbank merely steps away, pressing her fists to her face.

While my eyes were turned away, Miss Blake thrust the knife into my left shoulder and twisted it. Agony shot through my body like shrapnel and knocked me to the ground. She ripped the knife from my shoulder and stabbed me again and again. I clawed at my assailant, but my strength quickly drained from my body, along with my blood which dripped onto the snow.

Gasping, Miss Blake fell limply on the ground, cradling her wounded arm. "Lucia, help me!" she whimpered. "I . . . I can't get up."

"No, stay away from her," I tried to say, but it only came out as a pained snarl.

Lucia stood frozen on the riverbank, her glance shifting from me to Miss Blake as tears rolled down her cheeks.

"Lucia, help!" Miss Blake sobbed, sounding more desperate. "I *need* your help!"

The girl pressed her hands against her eyes, sobbing through gasping breaths.

"Lucia, *help!*" Miss Blake pleaded, now clawing her way toward the child. "Quickly, before she gets up again!"

I tried to crawl toward Lucia, but my legs buckled beneath me and I staggered back on the snow. Lucia fell to her knees, burying her face in her coat and continuing to cry. In one swift motion, Miss Blake pounced on the girl, using her good arm to wrestle her to the ground. She coiled her arm around Lucia's neck and squeezed. Lucia gasped for breath and struggled against the woman's grip, but to no avail. Miss Blake looked up at me, her eyes dark and burning with a wild and furious fire.

Every drop of blood left within me burned with rage and I sprang to my feet. I let out a howl and ripped my teeth into Miss Blake's shoulder. She shrieked as her arms fell limp. Lucia wriggled away, tumbled to her feet, and ran. Miss Blake twisted in my grasp and slashed her nails into my muzzle. I growled in pain and dug my teeth into her shoulder more deeply than before dragging her to the river's edge. I threw her into the foul waters, and they received her body hungrily, consuming her whole.

I collapsed to the ground, exhaustion completely overtaking me. I lay there panting, each breath more labored than the last. Moments passed, and my ears pricked at distant voices calling from the street. As I listened, I scanned the dense forest walls and saw Lucia slowly step out from behind a tree. She glanced over her shoulder in the direction of the sound, then tiptoed toward me.

I let out a soft growl. *Lucia, you're safe now.*

She paused for a moment. She looked at me, her brows knitted in a thoughtful expression, as if she somehow understood. She caressed my muzzle, stroking my fur with her small yet sure hand. She stepped closer and closer, until she knelt beside me and laid her head against my stomach. Her breaths were steady and peaceful, and before long, my own breathing matched hers. She buried her fingers in my fur, and in that moment, what felt like a light filled my chest and the shadow within me lifted.

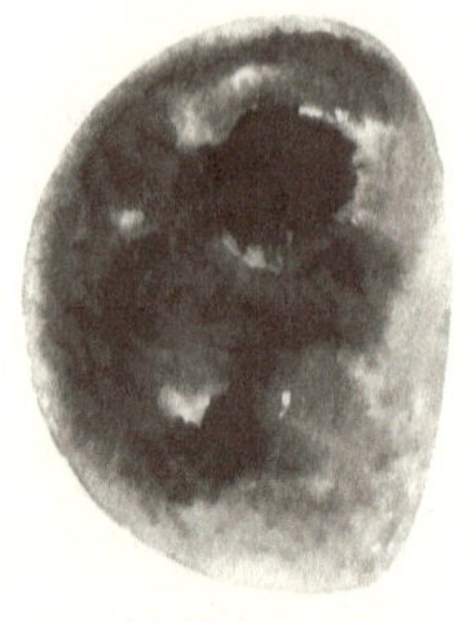

Wolfsbane

Anne J. Hill

A speck of pumpkin
A dash of spice
A pinch of souls
An ounce of doubt

A fist of fur
A cup of claws
A spoon of fear
And a douse of night

Stir in skulls
Mix in moonlight

Drop in shadows
Mutter the magic
Out comes a wolf
With the soul of a man

Mountains tremble
Rivers freeze
Leaves shake
For they got more
Than they bargained for

Such is the way
With Moonlight magic

Tumbling through towns
The wolf devours
Shifting to skin
When the time is right

He whispers lies
In the shadows
Stealing souls
To make him grow
But then he reaches
A village called
Wolfsbane

At the gate
A woman whose father

Raises the sun
Stands her ground

The wolf crouches
Ready to spring and
Swallow another town whole

But the woman whispers,
"No. You're not welcome here."
White light spills from her lips
Piercing through the darkness

The wolf laughs
Works his jaw
Ready to consume
Unready souls
But as he steps closer
The woman utters a message
To the Sun Raiser:
"Protect. Brighten. Save us."

The wolfman shudders
As the light of day
Banishes the shadow
Back to the darkness
From whence he came

And on that day
The world is free of

The shadow wolf
With a man's soul

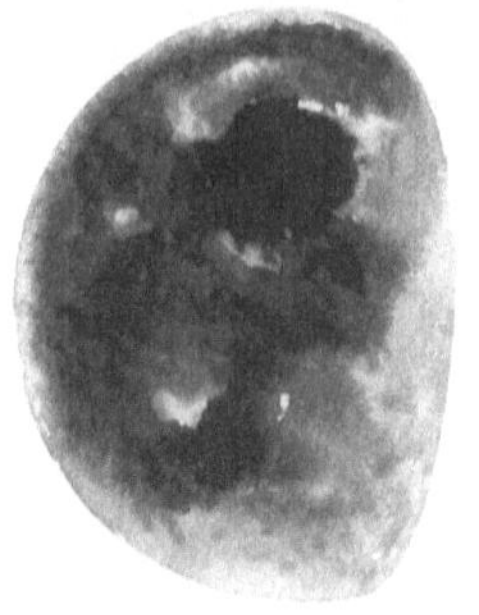

A Band of Silver

Morgan J. Manns

The thin silver band circling Lucien's neck began to tighten. Closing his eyes, he suppressed a sigh.

Not now, Rebecca, he thought through clenched teeth. *I'm busy.*

This happened often enough that it barely surprised him anymore.

He returned his focus to the physics lecture, scrambling to catch the professor's words.

"As we discuss the principles of aerodynamics, it's crucial to understand how Bernoulli's equation influences lift generation, allowing aircraft to overcome gravity and achieve . . ."

—Why are you wasting time learning these basic human philosophies, Lucien? Rebecca's consciousness flooded his mind, disrupting his focus. *It's beneath you now. And how you stand to be in a room with the humans for that long is beyond me. They all stink of*

stale dreams and corruption. We may protect them, but that doesn't mean—

It's not philosophy, Rebecca. It's physics, and just because you hate humans— He growled, pushing his pen into the paper with too much force. SNAP! An audible crack echoed through the quiet lecture hall as black ink spilled over his notes.

The balding professor stopped mid-sentence, turning from the whiteboard to stare at Lucien. Could the man's eyebrows go any higher? The other students in the room followed the professor's gaze, their looks ranging from incredulous to annoyed.

Lucian swallowed the lump in his throat that had nothing to do with the uncomfortable band around his neck.

Time to leave.

"Uh, sorry . . . Faulty pen." He forced an apologetic smile as he gathered his pride, notebook, and pen fragments, stuffing everything into his backpack in his haste to exit the room. He hoped that if anyone saw the metal band, they would just think it was a trendy piece of jewelry.

As the door rattled shut behind him, his teeth sharpened into points. He sealed his mouth into a thin line, wrestling to maintain his human form. With a steadying breath, he retracted the fangs.

He let his annoyance flow down the band back toward his Alpha. *Come on, Rebecca! Couldn't you leave me alone until the lecture was finished? I wanted to learn about that stuff. Your little interruption almost made me wolf out!*

Instead of a response, he received another pulse along the band akin to a small electric shock. With it, he got a quick image of her Lexus.

He winced, realizing she was already in the parking lot waiting for him. Another figure was with her.

Throwing the backpack he had stolen into the nearest garbage bin, Lucien stalked across the campus, readying himself for a different kind of lecture.

"Running off without telling anyone is suicidal, Lucien. The pack has to stick together or else the demons will find us. They're extremely good at tracking down lone wolves." Rebecca's voice held strong notes of criticism as she shifted her Lexus into a higher gear, the roaring engine driving them higher into the mountains.

Lucien worked his jaw and glared out the car window, barely listening. He chose to watch the forest of evergreen trees flash by in a blur, blocking her out. He knew the risks of being alone. He just didn't care.

A child's voice piped up from the backseat. "That's why Rebecca brought me along! I'm her shield. Nobody can see us." The child giggled. "I love road trips!"

Lucien couldn't help himself. His sneer twitched into a small grin. Dragna was the youngest of the pack, always cheerful, always ready to add her thoughts to a conversation. If Lucien had to spend time with any of them, the ten-year-old was his pick. She was the little sister he'd never had.

"That's right, Dragna," Rebecca said, turning the car around a tight corner. She threw a thought down the bond at Lucien. *Even the child knows to stick together.*

Lucien's small smile immediately disappeared. He turned toward Rebecca, glowering.

The Alpha had one hand gripping the top of the leather steering wheel, the other on the gear shift between them. Locks of raven hair tumbled around her shoulders over her black T-shirt, falling just short of her ripped blue jeans. She didn't look much older than Lucien, but Rebecca had been alive for over a century. A long life in a youthful body was a side effect of being one of the Changed.

He turned away and caught his reflection in the window. A flush crept up his neck when he saw the metal band with its constant reminder of the control Rebecca had over him. "Could you loosen this a bit? It's driving me crazy." He pointed at his neck.

She tucked a long strand of hair behind her pierced ear. "Hmm? Oh, yeah, sure."

The metal expanded and then fell lower on his neck. Releasing another sigh, he pushed a finger under the ring and massaged the irritated skin before letting it fall back into place.

"Thanks," Lucien grumbled, offering her a quick glance.

She nodded, sending a quick apology through the bond before diving back into her lecture, her words like grinding background noise. Dragna hummed to herself in the backseat, seemingly unaffected by the tension in the car.

He shifted under his seatbelt, again ignoring Rebecca.

If he could reverse time, he would. He'd go back six months ago and relive his graduation night. He would say no to that ridiculous dare from his classmates that almost got him killed. Taking his mountain bike to the top of a mountain and letting gravity take over—sending him off the path and into a gully—had almost killed him. Rebecca stumbling upon him that night may have saved him from dying, but his new life devoted to her meant he gave up his human one. Something he never would have guessed was possible.

Yet, here he was. One of the twelve Changed recruited by Rebecca to fight against the demons that were slowly infiltrating this world from a portal somewhere in the mountains.

Lucien gritted his teeth, frustration simmering beneath his skin. If only the demons didn't have the capability to shapeshift into humans and live among them unnoticed; perhaps then he could have lived a more normal life. But no. While the demons couldn't speak to humans, being near them infected the human heart with malice and hate, a poison invisible yet potent. This is why Lucien had been forcibly conscripted into this secret society of monster hunters by Rebecca. The other Changed seemed far more willing than he was to give up their humanity, embracing the monstrous burden he resisted with every fiber of his being.

Rebecca's voice broke through his thoughts. "Did you hear what I said?"

He hadn't. He had completely blocked her out.

She glanced briefly toward him before returning her amber eyes to the road. "Oh, stop your sulking, boy. You're lucky I found you when I did."

Lucky? That word broke something within him, and a low growl rumbled from deep within his throat. "Lucky! Do you mean I was *lucky* you tore me away from living out one of my dreams today, or was I *lucky* six months ago when you Changed me into *this*?" He gestured to his reborn in-human body.

She unleashed a growl of her own, her hands tightening on the steering wheel.

Dragna's humming from the backseat ceased.

Lucien clenched his jaw. He didn't want to argue with Rebecca in front of Dragna, but heat boiled under his skin. His wolfish emotions were at their breaking point. The words tumbled out faster than he could leash them. "Either way, Rebecca, I don't feel lucky at all. Losing myself to your cause was one of the worst things that has ever happened to me." He sat up straighter in his seat, his muscles flexing. Fangs sharpened against his lips, but he didn't bother to withdraw them this time.

Not in front of Dragna, Rebecca growled down the bond.

It's probably part of the reason Rebecca had brought Dragna to the University with her in the first place. She figured the young girl would help reign in Lucien's emotions. But there was no turning back now; he may as well let out all of his thoughts. He'd just say them down the bond.

You may have saved me by turning my broken body into one of the Changed, but you stripped everything away that made me, me! Now I don't know who I am or what my purpose is except to blindly follow you.

He leaned back in his seat, breathless at finally admitting everything to her.

Every word he said was true. He felt like he was walking someone else's path—not his own. If he had his way, he'd be attending a military college, studying to become a pilot, not stuck in the mountains with a bunch of wolves.

Just because Rebecca thought being one of the Changed was more important than a mortal life, didn't mean he had to think the same thing, too.

The silence stretched between them, and he almost regretted voicing his opinions. Dragna remained quiet in the backseat.

He wondered if Rebecca would have some sort of punishment for him when they reached the rest of the pack.

Two more bends in the road and she finally broke through the tense air with a sigh. "I know you miss your human life, Lucien. I feel it down the bond every day. You don't exactly hide your thoughts from me. You've likely always worn your emotions on your sleeve, even before I fitted your band." She nodded to his collar. "But together, the pack is stronger. You're a key member, and . . . We need you."

It was the closest thing to an open, real conversation Lucien had had with Rebecca. Although he was still furious, he could feel remorse through the bond. Saying the words aloud meant she wanted Dragna to hear it too.

He felt a little calmer. "Rebecca, I don't know why you fight so hard for humans. You don't even like them—"

Rebecca suddenly leaned into the steering wheel, glaring at the rearview mirror.

"Blasted bats." She pressed her foot down to the floor, shifting the car into another higher gear. The engine roared.

Dragna gasped.

"What?" Lucien turned in his seat, scanning the road behind them. At first, all he saw was the endless path of evergreen trees. Then, in the sky he noticed three black dots framed by mountain peaks, making their way towards them, getting larger.

"Demons," Rebecca said, cold fury blasting through the bond. He felt his skin ripple in response to her strong emotions.

He'd never seen one before.

Lucien reluctantly called forth a sliver of the wolf within him. His focus sharpened, everything becoming clearer, and he knew that his blue eyes had changed to gold with narrow pupils.

With enhanced sight, he could see the demons pumping their wide, membranous wings, propelling them toward Rebecca and Lucien.

"Do you think they know we're here?" Lucien growled low, wondering if the creatures could hear their car roar through the mountains from miles away.

Rebecca shot glances between the rearview window and the road in front of them. "There's no doubt, Lucien. They probably sensed you back at the college. You were alone and vulnerable," she snarled, turning the car around a curve, hiding the three figures from view.

Dragna whimpered.

"It's okay, Dragna," Rebecca said. "We're together now. They won't be able to sense us as easily."

Dragna's small voice spoke up. "I've never seen one before. I don't want to! They're scary!"

Lucien's hands turned clammy. He turned his attention to Dragna, keeping his voice cheerful. "With you here, there's no way they'd want to fight. You're the fiercest of the pack."

A small smile peeked out from between the locks of blonde hair covering her face.

Lucien smiled back, hoping his words had offered her some comfort. He turned forward and fidgeted with the band around his neck. If he could get this thing off, Rebecca wouldn't be able to track him. He'd flee and deal with the consequences on his own. Maybe the demons would follow him away from Dragna and the rest of the pack.

But Rebecca was the only one who could remove it. How could he convince her to get it off him?

Rebecca snarled. "We're out of range of the rest of the pack. We need to warn them." She pressed her foot on the accelerator, revving the engine around another curve. The trees flashed by in a whirl, mirroring the speed of his heartbeat.

Rebecca's wolf pack had been living a reclusive lifestyle in the mountains the entire time he'd been one of the Changed. He was surrounded by the other members, always. They slept in the same cave, hunted together at night, and walked the forest together by day.

Although he knew the risks of leaving the pack, it had been grinding his soul that he had zero alone time. That he had to be present at all times. He didn't even like being with his human family. Why would he want to be with this pretend one?

When he'd seen his opportunity to sneak away during an early morning hunt, he had taken his chance and loped down the mountainside. He'd changed back into his human form, hitching a ride with a burly bearded trucker who was making his way to the city.

"Okay, I get it. I messed up." Lucien let out a ragged breath. "What do we do now?"

"I've already signaled the others to keep together and meet us at the lake. We'll fight the buzzards off there." She shifted to internal thoughts. *There's no way we can bring down three of those beasts alone. We'll need the whole pack.*

"I'm ..." He tried to find the words to apologize. He hadn't meant to put the entire pack in danger. He'd only been thinking about himself when he left. He didn't believe his actions would affect the others so strongly.

"It's fine, Lucien. What's done is done. Now let's just get to the lake and—"

Something massive careened into the Lexus, clipping the front headlight, and threw their car into a spin.

Dragna screamed, and Lucien froze, his fingers clamped around the seat.

Screeching metal, squealing tires . . . and then a heavy impact into the side rail had them flipping through the air.

"Change, now! Both of you!" Rebecca shouted through the turmoil.

Lucien obeyed; the power from the band around his neck went hot with his eagerness to change. His skin tore away for the wolfish beast within him to emerge. As the car flipped along the guardrail, his hands fisted inward, becoming paws. His mess of dark hair lengthened to cover his entire body with a heavy coat of fur as strong as iron. His bones and muscles began to change, ripping apart his human anatomy for the strong, agile body of the wolf.

Behind him, Dragna let out a shaky howl.

The seatbelt held his wolfish body back as his face angled outward, a snarling muzzle emerging with razor-sharp teeth.

As his wolf form settled, Rebecca's consciousness echoed through his mind. It was always clearer when he gave way to the wolf within. *Brace yourself!*

The car skidded to a stop, upright, steam whistling from the engine.

He turned his head to see Rebecca hunched awkwardly against the steering wheel in her own wolf form. A low whine slid from her throat, and he could feel her pain flow down the bond. She was hurt.

Dragna's low whimper came from the backseat.

He opened his mind to the young wolf. *It's okay, Dragna. I've got Rebecca. Just get yourself out of the car.*

Dragna's small shape jumped through the broken window, landing outside the car.

Lucien scrambled from under the seat belt, nuzzling Rebecca with his muzzle. She barely opened her eyes, but he could feel her thoughts echo through his mind.

I didn't change fast enough, and . . . that last impact really slammed me. I need a minute . . . Her words were coming slow and strained through the bond. *Get Dragna to safety.*

He didn't have time to respond. Another slam from the side pushed them farther onto the guardrail. Lucien stretched his neck upward, trying to see over the crumpled dash. His fur stood on end. The front of the car teetered over a cliff, thousands of meters stretching below them.

Another impact and they'd be falling to their death, strong wolff-ish bodies or not. No one could withstand that.

Lucien gently lifted the scruff of Rebecca's neck with his teeth, feeling her limp weight slide out from under the seat belt. He crouched low and then slammed into the windshield with his back, breaking the remainder of the cracked glass, careful to protect his Alpha from the impact.

Something within him drove him to want to save Rebecca. He didn't know if it was his wolfish instincts or his own desire. Perhaps he just didn't want Dragna to see Rebecca hurt. She was the closest thing to a mother Dragna had now.

He landed on the hood with Rebecca before bounding them back onto the pavement of the highway. Behind them, the car teetered threateningly over the edge.

After laying Rebecca down gently near a rocky outcropping, he turned to get his bearings. *Dragna, where are you?* He swung his head, searching the empty road. What had slammed into them?

A piercing screech echoed through the mountain peaks. A pair of black wings churned the air around him like a storm, ruffling his midnight fur. He backed up, crouching low over Rebecca.

I'm over here. Lucien got a glimpse of a small rocky cave through the bond. Dragna must be hiding within the small cluster of trees along the roadside.

Get to the lake, he instructed. It was a couple of miles away. *Warn the others.* He unleashed a menacing snarl as he looked up toward the sky.

One demon circled above the treeline, casting shadows around Lucien. He didn't know where the other two creatures were, but surely he could handle this one.

Demons, spawned from the depths of the earth, were a natural-born enemy of the Changed. Where wolves stalked the ground, the winged demons owned the skies. The demons had one goal—destroy.

This wouldn't be an easy fight.

Lucien assessed the demon circling him like he was a piece of carrion. Its skeletal body was vaguely humanoid. Flying upright with two giant wings erupting from its back, it had elongated arms with talons in place of fingers. Its legs were muscular, and tucked beneath its body was a narrow spiked tail that swung at Lucien like a whip.

His stomach churned at the sight of the creature's head. Curved horns punctured through its gruesome bony skull, accenting the tiny black-beaded eyes set into its oversized face. A gaping mouth with razor teeth snapped at him. Every few seconds, the creature would open its maw and scream a battle cry in Lucien's direction.

Crouching low, his great paws sprung him forward. He bounded up the rocky outcropping in seconds and launched himself at the demon still circling above.

Rebecca had once said that the demons felt overly confident in the sky. Perhaps he could use that.

Lucien's powerful legs propelled him through the air, and he collided with the unsuspecting beast.

The demon pumped its wings desperately as Lucien used his momentum to sink his teeth into the creature's bony neck. It screamed, flailing its wings. Lucien's heart thundered against his chest as they fell in a cyclone of fur and claws.

The demon fought back and pumped its wings, keeping them from hitting the ground. Talons sliced into Lucien's flank like knives, and he jerked away, pressing off its body with his paws. Lucien snarled before biting harder into the neck of the beast. Sudden pain flared down his spine. The creature had torn into his back with its tail.

Agony ricocheted through him, hot and terrifying. He let go, falling through the air. He quickly angled his body around and landed on the pavement with his paws cushioning his fall. The impact jarred his bones, but his strong legs absorbed most of it.

He glared upward.

The demon screeched behind him. Lucien spun, ready for another impact. As he took a sharp breath, preparing for the attack, fur flashed past him.

Rebecca snarled as she slammed into the beast, crashing it into the ground.

The she-wolf attacked with a vengeance Lucien didn't know was possible. Even hurt, she was brilliant.

Lucien had been through training exercises with Rebecca and the others, but he'd never faced a demon before. Never witnessed the other wolves fight one.

Before the demon could right itself, Rebecca silenced its screams, tearing it to shreds with her teeth. Nothing could live after that.

Lucien's breath caught in his throat. How was she so powerful?

He reminded himself that she was the original Changed. Stronger than any of them.

She raised her head and turned back toward him, her breathing ragged but her eyes fierce.

Lucien gathered his strength and howled in triumph, his cry echoing through the mountains.

He opened his mind. *Rebecca, you killed it. It's—*

Watch out!

Another set of talons grabbed him by the scruff and yanked him upward. Lucien snarled, kicking out with his paws but finding only air beneath him.

Fur flashed above him again, and the demon released its grip on Lucien.

As Lucien tumbled across the ground, he lifted his head. Unbalanced from the pain wracking his body, he saw Rebecca biting hard into the demon's shoulder.

A guttural scream erupted from the beast, and Lucien's eyes widened in horror. The beast was falling into the ravine with Rebecca still holding onto it with her teeth.

Let go, Rebecca!

Just before the she-wolf and demon fell over the ravine, she released her hold. Fear lacing Lucien's thoughts, he watched helplessly as Rebecca fell beyond his view.

No! He limped toward the guardrail and peered downward. A distant figure lay at the bottom of the mountain among the trees. *The pack needed her. Especially Dragna.*

She couldn't be dead. She was their leader, the one who kept them level-headed. Together. Safe. Seeing her fight had changed something within him. Respect for his Alpha bloomed.

I'm here, Lucien.

His heart leaped in his chest. He turned his gaze to the side and saw her sprawled on an edge of rock, just over the edge of the guardrail.

The figure at the bottom of the ravine must be the demon. Dead.

He stared, a jolt of worrying, uncomfortable emotions looming in his chest. Blood covered most of her fur. He didn't know if it was hers or the demon's.

He felt a sliver of comfort when she spoke, even if her eyes remained closed. *Lucien, there were three of them. Where is the third?* Her thoughts were cloudy as she spoke to him through the bond.

Suddenly, a sharp, pained howl echoed through the mountains.

Rebecca lifted her head and opened her panicked eyes toward the sound. *That was Dragna!*

Lucien winced, imagining the young girl fighting the demon.

She's hurt, Rebecca whined. *The third demon found the pack at the lake. You need to go and help the others.* She paused, likely receiving a message from another pack member. *Haleh sent me an image. It's larger than the last two.*

Because Rebecca was so powerful, she could hold everyone's consciousness in her mind at great distances. Lucien was only able to hold one or two without garnering a headache. Rebecca claimed headaches only came to those who hadn't fully accepted the pack and that, with time, he'd come to accept everyone.

Lucien put his paws up on the guardrail, looking down at Rebecca with a new understanding of the creatures she had dedicated her life to defeating. He couldn't imagine wandering alone, encountering these beasts. Had Rebecca fought them on her own before she had her pack? Is that why she fought so hard to keep us together? He knew almost nothing of her history.

I can't leave you here. Who's supposed to lead us?

Rebecca peered at him with weary amber eyes, and he knew she wasn't up to fight. *Lucien, you can do this. Work with the pack, and you will overcome the darkness.*

Something twisted in his chest. Lowering his muzzle toward her, he said, *Okay, I'll go, but we're coming back for you when this beast is dead.*

The she-wolf closed her eyes again and rested her head on the ground. *May your claws be sharp, Lucien.*

He paused to take in her bloodied form, then nodded and ran toward the lake, ignoring the pain slicing through him. As he bounded across the forest floor, the silver band around his neck felt lighter, somehow.

Lucien shuddered as the thrill of the fight left him. He stopped at the edge of the forest and turned his muzzle to the wound in his side. Blood seeped through his fur, but he didn't think it was fatal.

He swallowed the fear racing through him and forced himself on toward the lake, his paws thundering across the ground. Instinct drove him, the minds of the other wolves a beacon in the distance. While he hadn't opened himself up to them fully—he dreaded the headaches and hated feeling others in his mind—their collective consciousness was enough to direct him.

As he neared the lake, the snarls and screeches from both the demon and wolves called him closer.

Racing across the damp earth of the forest floor, he emerged into a nightmare.

His packmates—six wolves with silver bands around their necks akin to his own—were scattered around the clearing, growling at the sky. At the center, a small prone wolf whimpered on the ground. It was Dragna. They were trying to protect her, he realized.

A push against his mind brought Lucien's attention back to earth. It was another wolf wanting to speak with him.

He breathed deeply, reluctantly opening the connection.

Reyla's voice slammed into him. Another senior member of the pack. *Lucien, what in claw's name took you so long? Where's Rebecca?*

He scanned the clearing, noticing the blonde she-wolf staring directly at him. Her pained yellow eyes sent a pang of regret through him. He noticed scrapes down her side and dark blood staining her fur. It reminded him of how he'd left Rebecca's bloodied form.

Reyla, it's a long story. She's hurt from fighting the other two demons alongside me. We need to deal with this one and—

The gargantuan demon swooped low over the lake, ignoring the snaps from the wolves, reaching to grasp Dragna and lurch her upward. Lucien's heart dropped as it carried her writhing form higher into the sky.

Lucien loped toward the other wolves, snapping at the sky in a fury of teeth.

Dragna!

Lucien, help! the young wolf cried through the bond.

The demon screeched back in response. Then, Lucien froze, the hairs on his back bristling as a small wolf fell from the blue heavens. He held his breath as Dragna's form splashed into the center of the lake, sending up a splash of water in her wake.

No! Reyna and the other wolves howled into the sky—a mournful, eerie sound. He snapped his bond closed, completely. Dragna's presence was gone. She was dead.

A growl reverberated from his throat. He hadn't realized just how connected he'd been to the young wolf. The pain he felt now drowned out everything else, eating at every inch of him. Dragna shouldn't have been away from the pack in the first place. She was dead because of him and his stupidity. He never should have left the pack. Never should have put her in such danger.

He glanced at the towering mountain peaks, grief swallowing him. He had to do something. The beast was still circling above them like a vulture.

A sudden idea came to him. Hope flared within his chest as he thought about the college lectures he had snuck into. There was a particular military tactic one of the professors had talked about . . .

He made a quick decision to open his mind to the other wolves, bracing himself for their combined grief, while trying not to think about how silent Rebecca's thoughts had become.

He was surprised when no headache emerged.

Lucien hunkered down behind a rock, taking note of the other wolves' positions. Haleh, Reyla and two others stood poised at the edge of the lake, howling in combined grief. Lucien scanned the skies, anticipation swallowing him whole.

Davik, do you spot anything from your position? Lucien asked down the bond toward the wolf hidden under one of the towering evergreens.

Davik's deep voice rumbled back toward him. *No, nothing yet, but it's only a matter of time until—*

A screech from the sky tore Lucien's gaze upward. The demon swooped low, just as Lucien had predicted when sharing his plan with the others earlier. With its large wings taking up most of the clearing, the demon had limited movements. It aimed its talons toward the four wolves near the water's edge. Lucien tensed as Davik sprang from the shadows, grasping onto the demon's leg.

The demon screeched, its cry high and pained as it arched back toward the sky. Lucien jumped from his rocky outcropping and latched onto the other sinewy leg, the combined weight of the two wolves pulling the demon down. It flared its wings desperately, sending gusts of wind across the clearing. Trees swayed dangerously while the other wolves inched their way across the debris-strewn ground, their fur bristling with combined apprehension.

Lucian could feel their wrath. Their desire to bring the beast down. It flared his own desire, and he clamped his teeth down harder.

When the demon was within reach, the wolves lept from their haunches and sank their teeth into the demon's sides. Another painful cry from the demon ricocheted across the clearing. The cry was so sharp, it could have cut the sky in two.

Lucien was flung sideways as the creature tried to shake him and the others free. His stomach rolled and his teeth ached. But he held firm, knowing the demon couldn't withstand the multiple wounds and the weight of the wolves pulling it down. The creature's movements began to slow.

In a few more heartbeats, Lucien could feel themselves lowering to the earth. When his paws touched the ground, he knew they had won.

The pack swarmed the creature, ensuring it would never rise again.

Although Lucien was proud of their success against the demon, he could not revel in the victory. Because of him, Dragna was dead. The grief still raw, he pushed his emotions to the side. For now, he was content that his Alpha still lived.

At Rebecca's request, he and the others remained in their wolf forms after the battle to partake in Dragna's funeral. This was the first funeral Lucien had ever witnessed, wolf or otherwise. The uneasy guilt coursing through him at the sight of Dragna's stiffened body threatened to eat him alive. He wanted to be anywhere but here. He wanted to run. But he wouldn't slight the young girl's memory. He would stay and honor her. It was the right thing to do.

Lucien and the rest of the wolf pack surrounded a pit dug by their own paws. Dragna, small and still, lay upon the newly dug earth, ready to be accepted back to the soil from which she had come. Her band had been removed by Rebecca. Lucien's tail was tucked around his body, his head low to the ground, mirroring the other wolves.

Rebecca limped onto a large flat rock, elevating herself over the pit. She was still injured from the battle against the demons but had insisted on leading the funeral.

When I first spotted Dragna near the waters of her home just four months ago, she was bold and daring. Rebecca lowered her muzzle toward the ground in remembrance. *She was jumping from rock to rock while her mother tended the garden. Dragna's giggles still echo through my mind.* Rebecca shared the memory through the bond.

Lucien's breath caught in his throat at seeing Dragna alive once again and hearing her laugh. Her blonde hair was tied into a ponytail, and a yellow-and-pink floral dress cascaded around her ankles. She was smiling. She was happy.

Hot tears stung his eyes.

Rebecca continued her story, and Lucien felt like his heart was about to be torn in two. *I was there because I thought another dark plane might open near the small mountainside town. Something just didn't feel right. It was like I was pulled toward this family and their home. I followed my instincts. Perhaps it was because I was meant to be there to help Dragna. Similar to how I came to all of you.*

Rebecca's disdain toward humans was normally so strong, so overwhelming, that it oozed down the bond into Lucien's own thoughts. She had mentioned more than a few times that she thought the humans were somehow responsible for inviting the demons to this earth. However, now, as she shared her image of the human family, Rebecca held no ill feelings.

She was simply . . . sad.

Although every wolf here had once been human, Rebecca never held it against them. She accepted them like family. Lucien had assumed it was because she wanted to grow an army against the demons and needed more wolves to do so, but perhaps this was more than just her desire to change humans. Maybe she simply craved a family of her own.

Rebecca continued. *I saw her slip. A mere second went by as Dragna laughed at a frog hopping alongside the riverbank, and then she fell to the rocks, the water swallowing her body whole.* Rebecca turned her head, her eyes closed. *I rushed toward her, but I was already too late to preserve her human life. Instead, I felt drawn to changing her.*

Lucien knew the rest of the story. Four months ago, when Rebecca returned with a wolf that was no more than a pup, she had told them the girl's lungs were too full of water, that she had been dying. And so, she had sunk her teeth into Dragna and changed her into a wolf to preserve her life. She'd become one of the pack.

Dragna was lost for a time, unsure of the wolves. Who could blame her? She was a young girl ripped away from the only family she'd ever known. As Rebecca spoke, Lucien tucked his tail in closer, guilty that he had done nothing to help, feeling too sorry for himself to think of anyone else. *But, as you all know, Dragna had a way of bringing people together. In a few weeks, she was scampering around the camp, nipping at the heels of the other wolves.*

The wolves shared in the memory, joy flaring through the bond. Lucien reveled in it.

She did not have the long life she deserved, but at least she was able to smell the fresh mountain air, chase butterflies, and find happiness in the extra time granted to her. Let us honor her memory. Let us always remember Dragna. Rebecca arched her back and howled into the sky. Lucien and the others joined with the mournful cry.

Rebecca had always changed someone close to death, who didn't have a hope of living. Lucien always believed it was because Rebecca wanted the new wolf to appreciate what she'd saved them from—life with her as an Alpha being preferred over death. But now, as they all howled into the crisp mountain air, he wondered if she was more reluctant to change people than she let on. Only doing so when she felt called to. He wished there was some way to save Dragna now.

As the howls filled the air, bleeding into the evening sky, Lucien realized that, for the first time, he didn't feel the tightness of the silver band around his throat. Instead, a fierce determination filled him as he glanced from Rebecca to his other pack mates. He wouldn't abandon them again. They were his military unit. His family.

He thought his destiny lay with the military, but it turned out he needed Rebecca to find *him*. His true place was here with the wolves. His expertise in airborne attacks could be invaluable in their fight against the demons.

Perhaps, Lucien thought as he unleashed another high, piercing howl into the night, they really did have a chance against the encroaching darkness—so long as they stood together, united against the shadows.

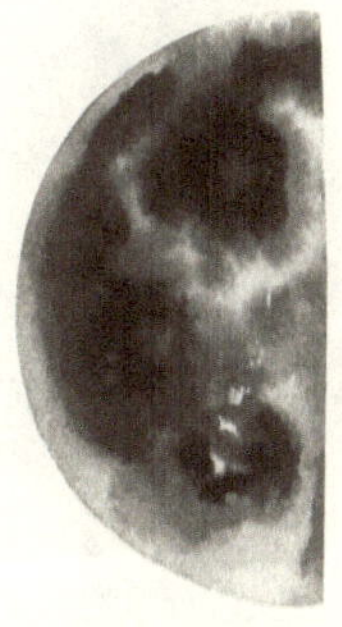

Waxing and Waning

Nathaniel Luscombe

The animal tide beneath my skin
obeys the ebb and flow
of the universe

I'm bound to the darkness
stretched between
the stars

w a x i n g

w a n i n g

changing form with the moon

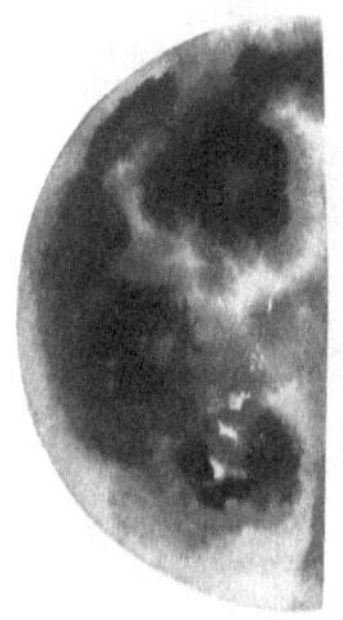

CLOAKED IN CRIMSON

AUDRAKATE GONZALEZ

The sound of distant howling jolted Lena from her position where she leaned against the balcony overlooking her kingdom. Fretian—a nation nestled amidst lush forests and green plains with spires that towered over the treetops—was where Lena called home. It was usually a place filled with joy and wonderment as merchants sold delicious foods, beautifully crafted pieces, and vibrant clothing for those who lived there.

But not tonight. There were no fires lit in the courtyard. No merriment in the streets. From her vantage point, everything looked so barren below. Her people—the young, old, and anyone not able to fight—were hidden underneath the city, safely tucked away. For now.

The howling grew louder. Closer. It was a sound that haunted her sleep every night since the *incident*.

Another howl broke through the sky, and a shudder rippled down Lena's spine. She rubbed the scar across her face, feeling the slightly raised skin that wrinkled her features. It still tingled under her touch, and seemed to itch at the sound of the wolves.

The Lycans had sent out their army. They were in search of a new place to rule, to spread their disease and create more savage beasts. They were all bloodthirsty monsters.

"Milady, they've moved their Alphas in. There's no way we can hold the line." The commander stepped onto the balcony. The whites of his eyes flashed, and sweat dappled his forehead despite the cool night air.

Lena's lips twisted. She figured that the Lycans themselves wouldn't show up to fight their own battle. Not when they had their Alphas, anyway.

Lena's own fear attempted to squirm through her bones as flashbacks threatened to rise to the surface. The wolves had taken too much from her already. She shouldn't even be queen—she was only sixteen—but she had no choice.

Lena beamed at her mother, who sat across from her in the carriage as they made their way down the King's Road. They were on their way back from celebrating a new peace treaty with the Kingdom of Elodia. One that would guarantee strong armies to face the Lycans. It had been a wonderful ball. The music that was chosen, the speeches given, and the dance that Lena got to have with the prince.

She'd felt so special. She even got to wear some of her mother's crown jewels.

Lena's mother smiled at her. Lena knew that she was her mother's royal princess, looking regal and grown up in the Queen's necklace at the age of thirteen.

Lena's father, King Xander, reached across her mother's lap to squeeze his wife's hand. This was a night of triumph. Of glee. They celebrated the defeat of another pack at the hands of another royal. A victory against the wolves was a victory for everyone. And with the help of Elodia's alchemists, Fretian would now be able to forge silver weapons.

The Lycans would learn soon enough that the Kingdom of Fretian was strong. Her family was sure of it.

A howl echoed nearby. King Xander peered out the window at the dark abyss above them, and Lena copied his movements. From what Lena had overheard about the Lycans and wolves, the full moon gave them their supernatural powers. Without it, the wolves couldn't shift.

"Speed up the horses," Xander shouted to the driver. The whip cracking against the horses' backsides made Lena want to cover her ears. Her eyes began to water, and she tried her best to keep the tears at bay, but a droplet of fear escaped and dribbled down her cheek. There'd be no reason to have the horses speed up if her father didn't think they were in some sort of danger.

Queen Georgette scurried next to Lena, scooping her against her side, a gesture that should have been comforting, but Lena could feel her mother shaking.

The only truly calming notion was the knowledge that there were coaches carrying guards both in front of and behind their carriage. Protection.

Lena let out a breath, but her heartbeat hammered like a war drum as the rhythmic pounding of paws hit the cobblestones. Those footsteps were gaining on the carriage. Lena shrank into her mother's side.

It will be all right.

It will be all right.

Lena chanted over and over in her head.

We have guards. We have each other. We will be all ri–

Screams like jagged knives tearing through delicate fabric broke out on all sides. A whimper escaped Lena, barely audible but full of vulnerability.

"Shh, my sweet child," her mother cooed, her own voice cracking. "It's going to be—"

The carriage was thrown, tumbling over the ground, over and over. Lena screeched as she was ripped from her mother's side by the force. The contents from dinner left Lena's stomach, spilling all around her. Lena crashed into the carriage door and flew out. She landed hard on the ground, the air ripped from her lungs, gasping as she tried to regain her bearings and pull herself up from the dirt.

On unsteady legs, Lena slowly rose. Her surroundings were pitch dark. She knew the wolves were there. Knew that their vision was unlike any other creature's. They could be watching her right now, a terrified girl, arms wrapped around herself, tears in her eyes.

"Mama?" Crying for her mother was the only thing Lena could think to do. She felt like a small child again, seeking out her mother to kiss her injuries and tell her that everything was all right.

She wandered back onto the road, something wet and sticky dripping into her eye. Most likely blood.

Snarling in the distance told her the wolves were up ahead. She glanced behind her in the direction of the castle. That was the direction she should run in, but she wanted her mama. *Needed* her mama.

Against her better judgment, Lena stumbled in the direction of the wolves. The belly of the beast.

The carriage lay in carnage on the side of the road. It would have been almost unrecognizable were it not for the mutilated horses that were still attached to the hitch.

Lena choked out a sob as she froze in fear, hearing the sound of teeth against flesh coming from just beyond it. "Mama?!"

A wolf jumped out in front of Lena, blocking her path toward the carriage.

From a young age, all children were taught about the wolves and the Lycans that created them. The Lycans—humans that were given a power called Lycanthropy from the moon goddess—were able to create beasts known as werewolves. These creatures were humans that could turn into giant wolves beneath the full moon.

But this wolf looked nothing like the werewolves from their stories. This wolf stood on hind legs, and was at least eight feet tall. She noted that the creature also had arms dangling at its side, and it didn't have paws but large hands with enormous claws.

Lena gave a quick glance to the sky. No full moon.

The wolf snorted as though it found Lena looking for the moon's fullness to be amusing.

"We do not need a full moon, child. We are Alphas. Created with no bounds." The Alpha took a menacing step toward her. Lena tripped backward, hitting the ground.

"Please, where's my mother and father?" was all she could say.

"Taking the forever sleep." He smiled, and anger flooded Lena's bones. Anger and something else that began to float to the surface of her skin. A spark of something . . .

The Alpha lunged closer, his putrid breath heating Lena's face.

"Please," she choked.

The Alpha tsked. "No survivors." He dragged his claws against her cheek. Lena threw her arm up in front of her and a bright silver light burst from her hand. It hit the side of the Alpha's face, charring it, and he screamed in agony, alerting the other Alpha's in their vicinity. He took off toward his pack.

"Talos has been attacked!" one shouted.

"Get to safety!" another snarled.

And then everything in Lena's world went black.

"How many?" Lena rubbed the scars on her cheek.

"Milady—"

"*How many?*" The Alphas were built strong, created with more power by the Lycans than the other wolves. Created by using demons in place of humans.

"At least a hundred." The commander's voice shook.

A hundred Alphas. Equal to at least a thousand soldiers in strength.

"Then it's time to send in the alchemists and mages." Lena's secret weapon. "Let's see how well the Alphas fare against magic."

Maybe it had been a mistake not sending them out first, but Lena was new to war, and she'd been hoping to keep their magic a secret from the Lycans for as long as possible. But it seemed as if now was the time to show them what they had been working on.

In the past, alchemists and mages were only used for medicinal purposes as they were deemed too important to risk in battle, but once Lena became queen, she knew she had to turn them lethal for the sake of the kingdom.

After the slaughter of her family, when Lena's own magic awakened, the mages were more than happy to help her harness it. But alchemy magic was different from traditional magic, granting the user power to transform matter and elements rather than manipulating energy by casting spells. This magic required Fretian to ensure Elodia followed through on the deal they'd made with Lena's father before his death. They would help her make a formidable army.

Elodia was home to many who studied alchemy magic, and with the treaty between the two kingdoms, they opened their gates to Lena for her training.

It'd taken months of practice, and gaining an understanding of chemistry and the natural world. The times that Lena felt like giving up were many, such as when she accidentally turned a goat into a silver statue and a master of alchemy had to reverse it.

But there were also glimmers of hope in her magic, like the time she learned how to weave patterns in the air, creating shimmering stars close enough for the people in her kingdom to touch. It'd brought them so much joy.

When Lena finally mastered her alchemy powers, it was time to turn all the mages into a force of ammunition.

Now, Lena lifted her hand, watching as a spark of silver danced across her fingertips. The Alphas despised silver, and Lena often wondered if there was some god or goddess out there that granted her this magic for this very day.

Donning her crimson cloak, Lena walked out to the drawbridge, the only entrance and exit into her kingdom. The mages, clad in their own crimson cloaks, stood waiting for her orders as the clash of weapons and cries of terror echoed beyond the kingdom gates.

"Tonight is the night we take back everything from the wolves. They cannot have this kingdom. We will destroy them beneath the full moon they worship. We will show the Lycans that their creatures have no place in this world." Lena pulled her hood up. "Crimson Cloaks, let's skin some wolves."

The drawbridge lowered. Lena barged across it with her army beside her. Bodies—wolf and human alike—littered the battleground. Lena's heart sank at the sight of men and women that she knew. Then she gritted her teeth. They'd died protecting her kingdom, and she would not let any of their deaths be in vain. Lena would make sure the wolves paid for every life they had taken.

The full moon cast an eerie glow through the thick canopy of trees. The wolves surrounded the kingdom on every side. Alphas flanked the battlefield, tearing through guard after guard, purging their way closer and closer to Fretian's gates.

With a swift motion, Lena conjured silver to her fingertips, forming barriers of protection around her mages and the entrance to her kingdom. These barriers were a trick she had taught herself. She'd practiced building the strength to hold them in the confines of her bedroom.

Blasts of light shot around her as the mages made quick work of the wolves. Howls echoed, but they were not howls of triumph; they were howls of terror.

While the mages took care of the werewolves, it was up to Lena and her group of alchemists to take out the Alphas.

She unleashed bolts of silver that struck with precision, repelling and killing the Alphas. Lena smiled as, one by one, Alphas fell to the ground, shock crossing their faces before they crumpled.

One Alpha took notice of Lena fighting in the middle of the battlefield and attacked her from the side. Lena landed roughly, biting her lip in the process. Blood dribbled down her chin.

She quickly rolled to her feet, hands back out in front of her, ready to release another wave of silver. But she froze.

The Alpha in front of her had a marred face. Marring that was created by her own hand.

Sparks flew from her fingers in response, excited to finish the job she'd started.

"I know you," he said, almost like a question.

Lena gave him a nod. "Talos."

He snorted, and he sounded just like he did the day he killed her parents.

Lena snorted back. "No survivors." She sent a blast of magic out of her hands, more powerful than she'd ever created before. The battlefield would only know silver by the time Lena was finished with it.

The wolves had turned her into a queen, thinking they would easily destroy her. But they had underestimated how sharp her teeth could be.

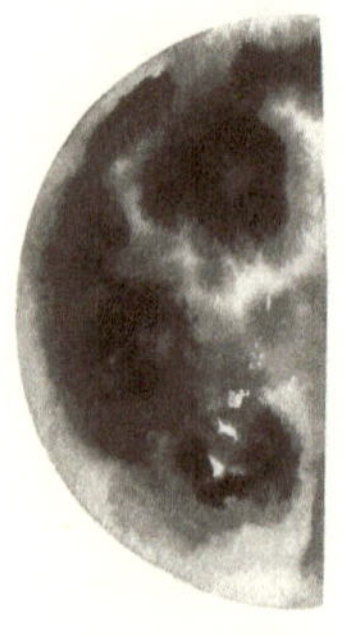

MOONBOUND

MIRIAM WADE

Wandering under the full moon's glow,
Eyes alight with a wild, untamed soul,
Roaming the night, a creature of lore,
Eerie howls echo, forevermore,
Woefully cursed, by the moon's control,
On a hunt, they seek their nightly toll,
Lunar metamorphosis, their secrets unfold,
Fearsome and fierce, a tale of old.

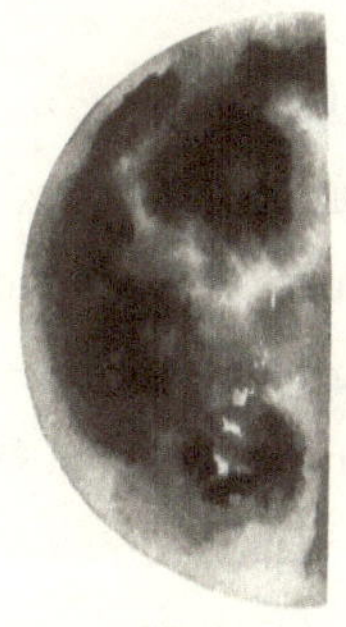

Payback and Popcorn

Crystal Bailey

My ride-or-die bestie, Fern, leans forward and opens the glove compartment to rummage through my snack stash. I take my eyes off the road just long enough to notice the hair on Fern's arms is already longer and thicker than it was when I picked her up an hour ago. She frowns when all she finds in the glove compartment are the fruit snacks, granola bars, and trail mix I keep on hand to satisfy my relentless snacking habit.

"Is this all you have to eat, Maeve?" she asks.

"I have some popcorn in the back, but I'm saving that for later."

Fern's disappointed frown turns into a look of disgust.

"Well, this is a pickup truck, Fern. Not a grocery store." I look back at the road just in time to swerve past an old lady in a white Cadillac going forty on the highway. I give the poofy-haired grandma a look of irritation through my window, then scold myself for being such a jerk. Normally, I'm not this impatient, but Fern and I have to make it to the woods before sundown, and the sun has already begun its descent.

Fern leans back against the passenger seat as a low growl escapes her lips. "Sorry," she mumbles, sounding ashamed. "It's just that I'm *starving*, and you know I can't eat that type of stuff right now."

I give Fern a sly grin. "Girl, I was just messing with you about the grocery store thing—you know I got you. Check behind your seat."

Fern twists around and opens the small cooler I placed behind her seat. She pulls out a plastic food storage container filled with raw ground beef, sets the container on her lap, and hastily peels off the lid. She scoops some red, bloody meat into her bare hands and shoves it into her mouth.

"That's grass-fed beef, by the way." My eyes are fixed on the road, but I hear Fern devour the raw meat like a wild animal. "Hey, be careful not to get any meat juice on the upholstery. My dad will kill me if I mess up his truck." It sucks that, as a high school senior, I still have to share a vehicle with my parents.

Fern finishes her nauseating snack and places the empty container back in the cooler. With a contented sigh, she pulls out her phone and scrolls through social media. My stomach does flip-flops when I notice her nails have become thick, long, and sharp. They will continue to grow at a rapid pace until they turn into deadly claws designed to rip through flesh. No matter how many times I've witnessed my best friend transition into a werewolf, I still can't get used to it.

Fern is adopted, so we have no idea if this whole werewolf thing is hereditary or not. I was the only person she revealed her shocking secret to when she first transformed about a year ago. It's still a secret just the two of us share, and I believe our long-standing friendship has grown stronger because of it. Though it can be stressful at times, having a werewolf for a best friend does have its perks.

For example, tonight we are on our way to a popular spot in the woods outside of the city, where we've heard a small group of Elites from our high school will be partying. Among this group of Elites will be two girls, Marnie and Poppy, who decided I should be their latest victim simply because I accidentally spiked the volleyball into Marnie's face during gym last week. The absurd rumors these girls have spread about me are a new low, even for them, though I give them points for creativity. If only they could somehow use their talents for good instead of evil.

Luck was on my side when I realized there would be a full moon on the same night as their party. That means Fern will be in all of her werewolf glory once the sun goes down tonight. I intend to take full advantage of this opportunity to extract a little revenge on Marnie and Poppy, along with their mindless minions who will also be in attendance and are just as bad as they are.

At first, Fern was reluctant to agree to my plan. She's a gentle soul who wouldn't hurt a fly, and I mean this literally because the girl can't even kill a bug without getting weepy. Then yesterday at school, this nerdy new guy, Tadd Covington—who I suspect has a crush on Fern—asked her about the latest lie Marnie and Poppy made up about me. He wanted to know if it was true that I was born with a small tail which I had removed freshman year and now keep in a glass jar on my nightstand. Fern saw how upset I was over this latest rumor, and, after giving her my word that no one would get hurt, she finally agreed to go along with my plan.

The plan is to scare these snotty Elites, not hurt them. Fern has amazing self-control for a werewolf. She never hurts people, but you should see what she does to bears and mountain lions. My stomach turns just thinking about it. Usually, on a full moon, I drive Fern out to the woods so she can hunt and devour large prey—the type of prey that's used to being a predator. She still has an insatiable need to hunt and feed during this time, which can't be ignored. So I promised to take her to a nearby remote section of woods where some hikers spotted a bear two days ago as soon as we complete our mission.

I pull off the highway and onto a dirt road, which leads to a clearing in the woods where teens go to do things they can't do at home. When I see the smoke from the Elites' campfire, I pull over and park in a spot behind some bushes that will help conceal the truck. Luckily, it still allows me a decent view of the action later.

As soon as I cut the engine, Fern opens her door and clambers to get out. The sun has just slipped away—it's almost time. "Full transformation will happen soon. I can feel it," Fern says with a faraway look in her eyes. When she speaks, I notice her canine teeth have turned into sharp fangs, and her ears have become longer and pointier.

"Thanks for doing this," I say.

Fern smiles at me; it looks unintentionally threatening. "No problem. Nobody messes with Maeve and gets away with it, right?" Fern's expression suggests she's more sure of this than she sounds. I hope she's not having second thoughts.

"Right. Just make sure they get good and scared. Like, wet-their-pants scared."

Fern's eyes widen as she shudders, then hunches over, gasping for breath. When she straightens, her fangs are even longer than before, and silvery gray fur has sprouted on her face and neck. "I don't think that will be a problem," she says. Her voice has changed. It's lower and gravelly.

Fern then creeps behind the truck and lowers herself until she's out of sight. She doesn't like for me to witness the final, most disturbing, part of her transformation. I respect her wishes and stay put. After a few minutes, I see a hulking figure completely covered in thick gray fur rise from the ground in my rear-view mirror. Fern's shift into a werewolf is complete. The normally petite girl is now a good two feet taller than before and has added on about a hundred pounds of solid muscle. Her claws and teeth are deadly weapons. Her night vision is as good as an owl's, and her strength and stamina far exceed anything a normal human could ever hope to compete with.

She's a total killing machine—but, lucky for us, she still has a heart of gold.

I open my door and Fern walks around to my side of the truck so we can speak. "Okay, Fern—it's go time. Remember, you have to work fast. Scare the crap out of them, then run back here and hop into the back of the truck and I'll take you to get some bear meat. Got it?"

Fern nods, then lowers herself onto all fours and sprints toward the Elites' vehicles, which are parked near the entrance to the campsite trail. She slashes every tire with her claws, just like we talked about earlier, so the Elites can't drive away. After the tires are taken care of, Fern looks my way one last time and releases a heavy sigh, her massive shoulders slumping, before she darts into the trees surrounding the clearing. Then I lose sight of her.

"Oh, this is going to be so good," I murmur, rubbing my hands together, giddy with anticipation. I roll down the windows and twist around to grab a pair of night vision binoculars and a large bag of popcorn from the back seat. Once I'm comfortable, I rip open the bag of popcorn and peer through the binoculars, chewing vigorously as I focus on the group of teens partying around the robust campfire. The light from the campfire illuminates each face, and I'm surprised to find an unexpected one among them.

"Tadd Covington?" I frown. "The nerdy new guy is partying with the Elites? How did he manage that?"

Fern, who is still out of sight, releases a long, eerie howl that pierces the still night air like a sharp knife. It's so terrifying that I even get goosebumps. "Nice touch, Fern." I smile and grab another handful of popcorn to shove into my mouth, never taking my eyes off the Elites . . . and Tadd. They all look around, petrified. A few of them stand and stare into the nearby woods, in the direction of the howl.

Then Fern emerges from the woods on all fours, revealing herself to the Elites. Her upper lip is curled up, and I assume she's snarling. The Elites cry out in terror. Fern stands on her hind legs, tilts her head back, and howls again. The Elites scatter, screaming and running for their lives . . . or so they think. A few of them head for their cars and then panic when they see the shredded tires as if realizing they have no means of escape.

Fern breaks into a run and chases the group around, paying special attention to Marnie and Poppy. In her werewolf form, Fern could probably outrun a cheetah, so she runs slowly on purpose to make it seem like she can't quite catch up with the humans. The Elites make a collective mad dash into the nearby woods, seeking cover. Fern follows them, and then flushes Marnie and Poppy back into the clearing for my viewing pleasure. She nips at their heels and howls, getting into the performance. Marnie's shrieks are almost as loud as Poppy's shouted expletives. At one point, Marnie stumbles and falls. Poppy notices, but abandons her friend with nothing more than a brief glance over her shoulder as she runs in the opposite direction.

I've never seen Marnie and Poppy lose their cool before. Overcome with delight, a devious giggle escapes my lips when I think of the recurring nightmares that will haunt them for years to come.

I grab handful after handful of popcorn as I enjoy the show way more than I probably should, pondering who else has wronged me in preparation for the next full moon.

After another minute, Fern stops giving chase and allows Marnie and Poppy to disappear into the woods with their friends. With everyone out of sight, and her mission now complete, Fern heads back to the truck.

Show's over.

I'm about to lower my night vision binoculars when I spot movement in the treeline behind Fern. Tadd Convington emerges from the trees, aims a small, strange-looking gun at Fern, and fires several silent rounds. Fern crumples to the ground, twitches, then goes still. My heart practically leaps through my chest and I feel as though I've been punched in the gut.

"Fern!" I scream, launching myself out of the truck, then sprinting as fast as I can toward my best friend.

When I reach Fern, I kneel beside her and examine her, expecting the worst. But there is no blood. No visible injuries of any kind. Her chest rises and falls with steady, rhythmic breaths. She looks as though she's sleeping.

Dry leaves crunch behind me as Tadd approaches. "She's not injured, Maeve. I used a tranquilizer gun, designed especially for werewolves. She'll be out for several hours, though." Tadd comes to a halt in front of me. When I look up at him, I notice his face is as void of emotion as his tone. He's all business, as if he's done this before. There's nothing nerdy about the new guy now as he hovers over me with an authoritative presence, tranquilizer gun in hand.

I stand to face him and notice several black trucks and a large black van with tinted windows pull up and park next to the Elites' vehicles. Mysterious people dressed all in black and wearing gas masks exit the vehicles and approach the clearing. Each person carries a weapon, and I doubt they are all just tranquilizer guns.

Tadd glances over his shoulder at the group, then turns back to me. "Don't worry. They're with me."

Yeah, like that makes me feel any better.

"What's going on, Tadd?" I ask, frantic. My eyes dart from Tadd, to Fern, and then back to the mysterious group approaching us.

"We've been tracking some new werewolf activity in this area. New activity usually means a local teen has turned because werewolves always turn between the ages of fifteen and seventeen. So the agency sent me here to go undercover as a high school student in hopes of uncovering the identity of the new werewolf."

"And you were able to figure out that Fern was the new werewolf you were searching for?" I ask, noticing Tadd's scary-looking friends are nearly upon us. One of them is pushing a large gurney.

Tadd nods. "I heard about this party out in the woods and scored myself an invite, which wasn't easy. But I knew any self-respecting werewolf couldn't resist a group of teens partying in the woods during a full moon and figured it would be the perfect time and place to capture Fern outside of the crowded city. But for some strange reason, Fern only seemed interested in scaring them, not attacking. Highly unusual werewolf behavior, I must say. When I realized no one was in danger, I contacted my team and told them to hold off on initiating capture so I could study this unheard of phenomenon for a moment. After Fern allowed Marnie and Poppy to run away, I gave my team the signal to move in."

Tadd's friends arrive in the clearing. Most of them form a circle around the perimeter and keep watch, but a few head off into the woods in the same direction as Marnie, Poppy, and the others. Four of them gather around Fern and load her onto the gurney. I move toward Fern on instinct, wanting to rescue my friend, but Tadd grabs my arm. A tall man wearing a gas mask, just like the others, approaches us and wordlessly offers Tadd a gas mask. Tadd takes it from him with a solemn nod. Then, without acknowledging me in the slightest, the tall man rejoins the others.

I try to yank my arm free as I plead with Tadd. "But Fern didn't hurt anyone—you said so yourself. It's my fault we were even here. Please, let her go!" My guilt is overwhelming. This is all on me. My petty need for revenge is what brought us out here, to these woods, where Tadd and his team were lying in wait.

Tadd doesn't release me. Instead, he uses his other hand to pull the gas mask over his head, then reaches into his jacket pocket and retrieves a small canister with a nozzle attachment. "I'm sorry, Maeve, but you won't remember any of this tomorrow." The mask muffles his voice, which makes what he just said sound all the more threatening.

Sheer terror causes adrenaline to surge through my body. Grunting, I struggle fiercely against Tadd, but can't break free. His grip is strong and immovable. Tadd aims the canister at me and releases a cloud of gas right into my face. I hold my breath, but can only do so for so long. When my lungs start to burn, I'm forced to suck in the tainted air. I cough. My eyes sting, and my brain muddles. My knees buckle. Tadd catches me just before I hit the ground and gently lays me on the grass.

With great effort, I turn my head to look at Fern as they wheel her large and limp werewolf form across the clearing toward the parked van. "What will happen to her?" I ask in a hoarse whisper, using every last ounce of strength I have left to do so.

Tadd's voice echoes as though coming through a hazy tunnel. "Don't know—that's above my pay grade. My job is just to capture them."

My vision blurs. I fight to stay conscious but feel myself slip away.

Then, darkness.

"Hey, wake up. I'm talking to you."

Someone is aggressively shaking me, but my head feels like it's stuck in a vice and my eyelids must weigh a thousand pounds—each.

"I said, wake up! What did you do with our phones?"

My eyes shoot open and I bolt upright into a sitting position when I recognize Poppy is the person speaking to me. The quick movement causes pulsating tendrils of pain to shoot down into my temples and behind my eyes. Wincing, I scan my surroundings and find I'm outside, sitting on the grass in the middle of a clearing near some woods. The sun's position in the sky tells me it's very early in the morning.

I twist around to look behind me and spot several Elites—some awake and moving about, while others lie on the grass, asleep. Or perhaps they're passed out; crushed beer cans and empty bottles are scattered all over the place. It almost appears as if someone intentionally went out of their way to make a mess of them. I never drink alcohol, so I know that's not the cause of the inexplicably murky morning I'm having.

So what *is* going on? What am I doing out here . . . and with the Elites?

Poppy repeats her question.

"I didn't touch anyone's phone, and I don't know what you're talking about." I reach into the back pocket of my jeans to check on my own phone, but the pocket is empty. Assuming I must have dropped it, I scan the surrounding area, but there is no phone in sight.

"Well, all of our phones are missing. And from the look of it, you've been out here partying with us all night when I know for sure you weren't invited. So what gives?" Poppy narrows her mascara-smudged, icy blue eyes at me. Her long blonde hair is disheveled and has a leaf stuck in it and her shirt is torn at the bottom. It's the first time I've seen her look anything other than perfect.

This time, I speak more forcefully. "I don't know, Poppy. I can't remember." Scanning Poppy's face, I find confusion, even fear, there. "I take it you don't remember much about last night, either?" She exhales and shakes her head.

Our revered, record-setting school quarterback, Slate, steps closer to us and chimes in, "None of us can remember anything after lighting the campfire last night. Must've been some rager we had, huh, bro?" Slate turns to one of his buddies, who expresses his agreement with a vigorous nod and thumbs-up gesture.

A loud groan diverts Poppy's attention. Maeve is lying on the grass several feet away and appears to be stirring. Poppy rushes off to attend to her friend.

Now that I'm more alert, the thought strikes me that I have to get home before my parents get out of bed. They'll kill me if they notice I'm not in my bedroom and realize I've been out all night. And they'll be worried sick. No doubt the first thing they'll do is call Fern, looking for me, and then she'll be worried sick, too.

With some effort, I stand, and once the earth stops spinning, I try to focus. What is the last thing I remember? Think, Maeve!

I was driving. Yesterday evening. But where was I going? I was on my way to . . . to . . . to pick up Fern! Yeah, that's it. I was going to pick up Fern, and we had plans. Plans to do what, exactly? Try as I might, I can't remember anything else.

Angry shouts erupt near the edge of the clearing. Two Elites—a stocky jock nicknamed Brutal and his stereotypically stunning cheerleader girlfriend, Anya—run toward us, yelling something about tires.

"Somebody slashed all of our tires," Brutal reports when he reaches us, his massive barrel chest heaving as he tries to catch his breath. "We're stuck here."

Marnie begins to sob. Anya points at me and says, "I bet *she* did it." Everyone stares at me.

My eyes dart from face to face. I take a step back. "I didn't do it."

Poppy crosses her arms and smirks. "Yeah, right."

"Wait a minute, wait a minute—I think Tail Girl might be telling the truth," Slate says, managing to insult me even as he comes to my defense. "That new kid, Tadd Covington, where is he? Dude was out here partying with us last night, and now he's nowhere to be found. I'm thinking he slashed the tires and stole our phones after we passed out, then took off."

The Elites all begin chiming in with their opinions and theories, but I drown them out because the mention of Tadd's name seems to have shaken something loose from the depths of my memory banks. I'm rocked by a sudden memory flash. In it, I see something large—I can't make out what it is—lying on a gurney being pushed by shadowy figures dressed in black. Tadd is speaking to me, though I can't see him, just hear his voice. He's saying something about how it's his job to capture them.

I squeeze my eyes shut, willing my brain to focus, to extract more from this memory. The images become clearer, and then grief-induced panic jolts through me when I realize the thing stretched out on the gurney is Fern in her werewolf form.

My eyes shoot open. Our plans! I remember now! It was a full moon, and Fern and I planned to come out to the woods to give Marnie, Poppy, and the others the scare of a lifetime because I wanted revenge. But something must've gone terribly wrong. Based on what I'm seeing in the flashback, Fern was captured and Tadd had something to do with it.

I break into a run, heading for the parking area. I don't remember how I got here last night, but it makes sense that I would've driven myself. Therefore, I assume the truck is parked somewhere nearby but out of sight. The Elites shout after me, wanting to know where I'm going. I ignore them and keep running until I reach the parking area.

A brief look around reveals a cluster of tall bushes not too far away. Hints of blue peek out from between the branches and leaves. My dad's truck is blue. I sprint over to the bushes and find the truck parked behind them. Luckily, the windows are rolled down; I don't have my keys. I open the door from the inside, slide into the driver's seat, and then frantically search the vehicle for my purse. I spot it in the back seat, behind an empty, crumpled bag of popcorn. Pushing the popcorn bag aside, I grab my purse and pull out the keys, tears welling up in my eyes.

This is my fault. Whatever happened to Fern is all my fault. I'm to blame for this. I pound the steering wheel with clenched fists as tears stream down my cheeks, then hang my head and sob, shoulders shaking. For all I know, Fern is being tortured right now, or experimented on. Or maybe . . . maybe she's already dead.

No! I can't think that way. I have to have hope that she's okay, that I'll find her somehow, even if it means putting my own life in danger. I start up the truck with trembling hands, maneuver around the bushes, and then speed down the dirt road that leads to the highway, leaving a trail of dust behind me.

Springing from somewhere deep inside, sudden rage and fierce determination courses through me, overshadowing my grief and guilt and putting an instant stopper on my tears. I wipe the last of them off my cheeks and grip the steering wheel with firm, steady hands as I make a silent promise to myself: I will find Fern—no matter how long it takes or what I have to do. I'll hunt down Tadd Covington and force him to give me answers.

Then I'll make him pay.

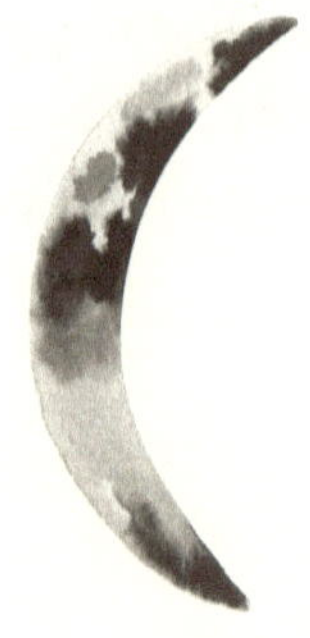

Moonlit Confrontation

Miriam Wade

Werewolf and Vampire in Verse

In the ancient dance of night and day,
Two beings clash in an eternal fray.
One, a creature of elegance and grace,
The other, a beast with a feral face.
Beneath the stars, their conflict unfurls,
A werewolf's growl, a vampire's swirls.
Their feud, ancient as time, rages on,
For in essence, they are night and dawn.

Beneath the moon's gentle light I roam,

A creature of nature, finding my home.
Your cold embrace, a mockery of life,
Feeding on others, endless strife.
You shun the sun, the warmth it brings,
While I bask in its glow, as nature sings.

In the dark I find solace and might,
A creature of elegance, born for night.
The moon's hold on you, a relentless chain,
Forcing transformation, causing you pain.
You claim to be wild, a part of the earth,
But my immortality grants a higher rebirth.

Your elegance hides a thirst for blood,
A parasite's hunger, a crimson flood.
I embrace my nature, my instincts true,
While you mask your hunger, playing the rue.
You avoid daylight and its life-giving grace,
A symbol of life, you're a twisted case.

Your connection to nature is wild and crude,
Bound to the moon, savage and rude.
The sun may shine, with life's fleeting glare,
But in darkness I thrive, with eternal flair.
Your howls and growls may echo your plight,
But I, immortal, transcend day and night.

As the stars twinkle above, they part ways,
Neither conceding in this eternal haze.

The werewolf's howls fade into the night;
The vampire retreats until hidden from sight.
Their paths diverge, their conflict unresolved,
Bound by their nature, forever involved.
Each to their own realm, they journey on,
In eternal discord, until the break of dawn.

Vox the Mastermind

Anne J. Hill and Hannah Carter

Ah. What we have here is a 12th-century Count van Droff original. As you can see by the delicate strokes, he was actually . . . blind. And paralyzed. He had to use his mouth to hold the paintbrush, and—"

Static crackled in Vox's earpiece, and a feminine voice barked, "*Vox.* I need you to shut up right now. Thank you. Just lead the group to the next painting, and for the fiftieth time, keep your fanging vamp mouth *shut.*"

Vox cleared his throat and cast the group of art gallery patrons his most endearing smile. "Yes. Right this way, if you will. The gallery tour will continue right around the corner, where we have a fabulous collection of paintings by the illustrious Lady Bissletoe."

"Lady *Busselton*, Vox!" the voice in his earpiece rang. "We went over this a thousand times. If you can't remember the facts, then stop talking. You'll blow our cover."

"I will not blow our cover, Mei," he muttered back. The crowd—full of rich, snobbish vampires—tramped ahead, and Vox took a moment to adjust his satchel and smooth back his voluminous black-and-white waves. A younger woman from the group lingered, and he winked at her, pleased at the blush that reddened her cheeks before she scurried into the next room.

Honestly. Sometimes, it astounded Vox why *he* was not on display at an art gallery.

"*Vox*. Get your butt into the next room!" Mei growled.

He clucked his tongue. "Temper, temper. Don't let it get the best of you, or else you'll go full wolf too early."

Her low rumble—a sure sign she'd probably started shifting into her werewolf form—morphed into a tired sigh. "I should have gone in. I knew it all along."

"Well, one of us is a wanted criminal after the *last* little debacle, and one of us got away scot-free, like the mastermind he is." Vox strode underneath wide marble arches into a room with a vaulted ceiling. A crescent moon shone down on the masterpieces inside—including Vox.

"*I* saved your little ungrateful—oh, never mind. Do you have eyes on the painting?"

Vox had eyes on *many* paintings, as a matter of fact. Each portrait in this room depicted royal vampires throughout the centuries, all painted by Lady *Busselton*. Since, of course, the vampire artist had lived through hundreds of dynasties. "I do."

"Good. Then just . . . keep quiet. Stay low, and please, please, *please*—don't blow our cover. I'm begging you."

Vox smiled. He would never blow their cover. He was a world-class actor, a real genius. He'd mapped out his plans from beginning to end and end to beginning at least a dozen times.

Several of the patrons whispered amongst themselves. One man lifted his glass of blood to cover his mouth as if that would keep Vox from hearing his words. "This tour guide must have been born yesterday."

Ah, yes. He was complimenting Vox's youthful nature. How kind.

While the patrons admired a painting of Countess deLu, Vox's eyes were on the portrait of a vampire duke who looked more like a corgi stuffed in a ruff.

"Can you see this, Mei? If I were the owner of this, I would want it to stay missing," Vox muttered. "Why would the gallery steal this in the first place? I could scarcely sleep with this in my house, even if it *was* my great-grandfather."

"Vox, nobody asked you for your opinion." Mei sounded exhausted. She often did, even though she drank at least a gallon of coffee every day, which still wasn't—according to her—enough to put up with his presence.

He understood. Being in the shadow of such glorious charisma *would* be a burden to anyone, especially an old tired dog like Mei.

"Shame these art critics don't ask for my opinion more. I would tell our . . . ah . . . *employer* that he is much better off without his dear old granddad's visage depressing his house's value. This man is in *stockings* and a dress."

Mei sighed, and a long slurp sounded in his ear. That must have been her fifth cup of coffee already. "Depreciating, Vox. The word is de-pre-ci-a-ting. And besides, that outfit was in style. Duke Hollinger would have been considered a very attractive man in his time."

Vox scoffed. "Attractive to a poodle, maybe, but not any woman with *taste.*"

"Someone's a little jealous, aren't they?"

"Excuse me, Mister Lox." A petite older woman with wispy, coiffed white hair shuffled over to him. What a pity she'd been turned at such an advanced age—it would be a bother to live with eternal arthritis. "Can you tell me about the history of that fine statue over there? The brawny werewolf one." She gestured to one of a man—who was thankfully hairy due to his werewolf transformation, which spared the world from being subjected to his nakedness.

"Ah. Yes. That is . . . Lady Mei Mei the Third, one of the last great werewolf leaders before the Moonlight Wars, where werewolves were stripped of their territory and the vampires took over as the ruling class. Historians tell us that Lady Mei Mei was at least partially to blame for the werewolves' devastating loss. She was, in fact, a terribly lazy leader. Left everything up to her prime minister . . . Box."

Mei growled. "Yes, and *Box* was incompetent, rude, self-absorbed—"

"Box was reputedly the most handsome man to ever live, you know. The exact opposite in every way of Lady Mei Mei the Third, but even he could not overcome her shortcomings and save the werewolves."

The granny adjusted her glasses, squinting at the figure. "A woman, you say? I could have sworn that was a man."

Vox nodded. "Yes, Mei Mei's story is quite tragic. Most people assumed that. She never did have a suitor." He clucked his tongue and swiveled back toward the painting of the corgi in the puffy suit—oh, excuse him—*vampire duke*, though his heritage did seem dubious.

The granny scrunched up her nose. "I don't recall any of this, and I was turned centuries before the Moonlight Wars. Where did you learn this?"

Vox leaned in and whispered, "In the dark caves of Mount Dracula. Deep, deep down where the bats tell tales long lost to the vampires beyond." He patted her cheek. "No one has ever ventured there, except for me, of course. So don't bother fact-checking. And I will not disclose the exact location because it's sacred. Now, may I suggest getting yourself a nice glass of blood and perusing the Verninhand collection on the *other* side of the gallery?"

She pushed out her lower jaw and narrowed her eyes at him. "All righty." She backed away slowly, showing her fangs ever so slightly.

Vox waved and turned back to his very important ugly painting. He'd clearly convinced that elderly woman nothing sketchy was going on here. Ah, what a mastermind he was.

"Now?" he whispered to Mei on the other end of the earpiece.

"Cameras are off, yes."

Vox cracked his knuckles. It was time to commit the best heist ever seen in all of North Sylvania. He flipped open his satchel and ran his fingers over the rolled-up canvas inside. Any moment now . . .

Shriek. "Wolf!" someone yelped.

A vampire careened around the corner and smacked right into Vox. "Werewolf!" The vampire grabbed Vox's face and screamed as if Vox had missed the commotion.

"Ah. Oh. No. Whatever shall we do!" Vox proclaimed as he shoved the vampire off of him. "Oh, dearie me, oh my . . . We better all run."

On the vampires' heels came the snarling, bristling giant that was Mei in werewolf form. Her large shoulders crashed into the painting of Countess deLu and cracked the frame. Mei tilted her head back and howled to the high heavens before chasing a vampire to the other side of the gallery.

"Oh, no. Better chase the rabid werewolf . . ." Vox clutched at his chest and gestured wildly to the few remaining patrons. "Or run away." When they simply stood and brushed themselves off, panting, Vox threw his hands into the air and screamed, "*Ahhhhh!* Run!" He darted toward the exit. Somehow, that was enough to get the remaining patrons outside into the night air. They barreled past him, leaving him behind.

Finally alone, he slipped back over to Duke What's-His-Face. Vox pulled out his knife and carefully cut the edges of the painting out of the frame like he'd seen in the movies—where all great masterminds got their training. He quickly rolled up the abhorrent painting and stuffed it in his satchel.

Now, to replace it with something worth looking at. With a piece so handsome no one would even miss this doggy duke.

Vox pulled out sticky tack and broke it into four pieces, balling each piece up and pressing his thumb into it. Then he beat the new painting onto the wall with his fist until it was properly attached to the adhesive.

He took a step back and placed his hand over his heart.

Marvelous. It would bring a tear to anyone's eye.

His work completed, Vox swaggered out of the gallery and into the open air. He could hear Mei's barks from down the street while frantic vampires rushed to and fro to escape the rabid monster. No one bothered Vox as he climbed into his van, started it, and drove down to the alley where he and Mei had agreed to meet.

Mei bounded into the alley, and Vox opened the window so her wolf form could leap into the seat. Once settled, she shifted, slamming the door. "Go, Vox. *Go!*"

The tires squealed as he accelerated and left the busy city behind.

"Did you get the painting?" Mei shoved her long, mint-green-colored hair out of her face. She'd dyed it a few days ago, an ill-advised attempt to disguise herself after her wanted photo had been plastered all over the news.

"Of course. How incompetent do you think I am?" Vox sniffed.

Mei glowered at him. "You don't want me to answer that." She dug through his satchel and sighed once she touched the painting. "All right. We did it. Now, all that's left is to give this back to its real owner and get paid." She paused, and she almost sounded *pained* as she muttered, "Good job, Vox."

He smiled, smug as a cat. "Thank you, Mei."

"Although you did almost ruin everything with your made-up art trivia. And *Lady Mei Mei*?" Mei rose and stumbled to the back of the van, which housed her remote computer lab. "Really, you've had some bad ideas, but—" Her voice cut off with a scream. "*Vox!*"

"What?" Vox slammed on the brakes and whipped around in his seat. "Are you all right?"

Red-faced, Mei glared at him with the fury of a thousand suns. "*What* is *this*?" She swiveled her computer screen around. The security camera revealed his masterpiece, as beautiful as ever.

Painting-Vox lounged on a recliner, dressed in a crimson vest, white shirt with puffy sleeves, and tight black breeches. He held a glass of blood in one hand as if to invite the onlooker to come and drink with him. His tousled hair fell perfectly across his face, his sultry pout on display for all eternity.

"You scared me, Mei." Vox let out a breath and pressed the gas again. "That's the replacement, as requested. The mission is complete."

"You were supposed to hang up an exact duplicate of the duke's portrait! I gave you the replica this morning!"

"Do lower your voice, Mei. No need to wolf out." Vox turned the van around a corner. "We both know that the portrait was *so ugly* that it had no right being on display at a gallery. I did the curators a favor and switched it out for something much more pleasurable to gaze upon."

"Vox! This is *evidence*! You just told the police who stole the painting. You're going to be a wanted criminal like me now!" Mei dropped her head into her hands and let out a feral screech. "We're going to have to go back."

"We can't go *back*!" Vox said indignantly. "Do you know how much I paid for that?"

Mei lifted her head. A low growl filled the air, and tufts of fur sprouted along her neck and face. "How much did you pay for that, Vox?"

He swallowed. "Um . . . ten thousand rubies."

Mei's screams reached a level that only dogs—or perhaps her fellow werewolves—could hear. "Vox! That's more than we're getting *paid* for this job!"

"This was a necessity!" Vox's voice rose as well. "That ugly stuffed corgi of a man could not be allowed to besmirch this art gallery any longer—"

"He's a beloved historical figure, and he does *not* look like a corgi!" Mei pointed a hairy finger back the way they'd come. "Go back, Vox. Go back right now!"

"This is an insult. My painting is a masterpiece, and you are depriving the people of my glory." Vox pulled off into a refueling station and turned around. "Modern art will suffer for your selfishness."

"I'm keeping your sorry butt out of prison, though I don't know why." Mei sighed. "Now I've got to delete this security footage, too. You couldn't just stick with the plan? For *once*?"

Vox cleared his throat. "I *did* stick with the plan. *My* plan."

Angry keyboard clicks sounded from Mei's computer. "I hope you know I'm never working with you again."

Vox flashed her a fanged smile in the rearview mirror. "You say that every time. Come on. Admit I'm a mastermind." He winked.

As they drove back toward the gallery, Mei grumbled, "Yeah, if by *mastermind* you mean 'Vox, the super incompetent vampire.'"

The Dark Things

Ali Noël

Is there hope for the dark things?

We creatures of the night

Yes, the ones who long to settle beneath the midday sun

Condemned to wander the light-forsaken stretches of nighttide

Doesn't the world know?

Why can't they see?

We fear the dark as much as they do

Night after dream-deserted night, it comes for me

This transformation I do not want

This burden I cannot bear

A buckling, a hounding

Agonizing me to the bone

And yet, dawn after dawn morning meets me
cloaking me with its gentle sun-risen hand
Breathing into my wearied lungs, my fatigued spirit
Declaring, *the night cannot last forever*

Acknowledgments

Thank you to the team of editors, beta readers, authors, and so many more people who poured their time and energy into this book. Thank you Beka Gremikova, Ellaina Ruse, and K.C. Lannon for edits, and shout out to Moriah Chavis. Thank you to our team of beta readers, Ali Noël, Natalie Noel Truitt, Brooke J. Katz, Aisling, and Rynn Ely.

- AudraKate Gonzalez, Anne J. Hill, and AJ Skelly

SIMILAR TITLES

If you enjoyed *There Will Be Wolves*,
checkout these books by Twenty Hills Publishing:

The Man of Twists and Turns
Briars & Blood
What Darkness Fears

UPCOMING FROM TWENTY HILLS

Meet the main characters of Morgan J. Manns' upcoming novel through Twenty Hills Publishing:

I t'll never work, Jake. Nobody could ever pull this off." The harsh tone behind her words sounds foreign to her ears. Somewhere in her mind, Skir chuckles.

She withdraws her hand, covering her mouth. *Annoying demon.* Skir is getting stronger the longer he lives within her.

They've tried everything to get rid of Skir and Scepta. They can't seek help from their professors for fear of execution once their curse is revealed. Instead, they have to pick their way through old scrolls, looking for myths about creatures long thought dead. Through sheer luck, they stumbled upon one that mentions the amulet. It seemed like their only hope.

Jake winces, his lips curling in a near-grimace. She half-anticipates a growl, but he merely shakes his head and offers a wry smile. "Seems like Skir is really under your skin tonight, huh? And breaking into a decrepit graveyard for an amulet may not be as breezy as it sounds, eh?"

She scoffs, crossing her arms, but a small smile edges at her lips. "Ghoulish guards, ancient magic protecting tombs, and removing an amulet from a dead guy's neck? Yeah, not so easy."

It feels good to banter like they used to. Lately, everything has felt entirely too serious.

His grin widens. "I'm sure the dead guy won't mind if his amulet takes a permanent vacation. And . . ." He reaches into his pocket and reveals a gilded chain with a half-moon-shaped pendant dangling from the end. "We already have the first key to ensuring this plan will work."

Her mouth drops open. "Where did you get that!?" It's half of an amulet, half of what they need to break the curse. The amulet looks exactly like the description they read about on the scroll.

As he begins to respond, fiery heat races across her skin. She gasps, pain flooding her vision as she falls to the floor, barely registering that Jake has done the same. He convulses next to her, unhinged.

Not again!

She manages to look out the window as the moon reveals itself from behind the clouds, full and terrifying.

The walls within her mind crumble, and Skir breaks loose. He howls triumphantly as her bones break and reform. She screams, her muscles stretching and fur growing across her body.

Skir's shadowy thoughts fill her mind. *Ah, I finally get to come out and play . . . Now, let me see. How do I ensure you never get your hands on the other half of this amulet? The next few hours should be incredibly fun . . . Nighty-night, Anna.*

In her last human breath, she swears never to surrender to Skir's tyranny again.

Her life has been taken from her.

Now it is time to take it back.

Keep an eye out for Morgan J. Manns' upcoming novel, which features Anna and Jake. Publishing through Twenty Hills Publishing.

About the Authors

AudraKate Gonzalez started writing horror stories when she ran out of Goosebumps books to read as a child. Her love for writing grew and now she has a BA in Creative Writing and is working on her MFA. Her YA/Horror Series, *This is Noir*, is available now wherever you buy your books. She lives in Ohio with her handsome husband, and her adorable furry bad boys, Zero and Scrappy Doo. When AudraKate isn't writing, you can find her reading, watching scary movies or sleeping.

Instagram: @lets.get.lit.erature
www.authoraudrakategonzalez.com

Anne J. Hill is an author who enjoys writing fantasy for all ages. Her love of words has led to her career as an editor and content writer. She runs Twenty Hills Publishing with the help of her circus-performing best friend, Lara E. Madden. She spends her days dreaming up fantastical realms, researching ways to get away with murder (for writing purposes), arguing over commas at the kitchen table, talking out loud to the characters in her head, promising her housemate that she isn't, in fact, crazy, and rearranging her personal library—affectionately dubbed the "Book Dungeon."

Instagram @anne.j.hill.editing

Twitter @AnneJHillAuthor

www.annejhill.com

AJ Skelly is an author, blogger, and lover of all things fantasy, medieval, and fairy-tale-romance. And werewolves. An avid reader and a former high school English teacher, she lives with her husband, children, and many imaginary friends who often find their way into her stories. They all drink copious amounts of tea together and stay up reading far later than they should.

Instagram @a.j.skelly

www.ajskelly.com

Nathaniel Luscombe is an author from Ontario, Canada. He primarily writes science fiction, but many of his projects fall under a sub-category called science fantasy. Between 2020-2023, he did a lot of self-publishing and anthology work. At the end of 2023, he signed several contracts with Dragon Bone Publishing. He is now co-running Dragon Bone Publishing with Effie Joe Stock.

Beka Gremikova writes and dreams from the Ottawa Valley, Ontario, Canada. She is the author of several twisty fairy tale retellings—"The Other Cinderella" and "The Spindle Trap"—and her short story collection, *Unexpected Encounters of a Draconic Kind and Other Stories*, is available now with SnowRidge Press. When not writing, you can find her travelling, geeking out over folklore and myth, and playing video games such as *Honkai Starrail* or *The Legend of Zelda*.

Hannah Carter is just a girl who still wakes up every day hoping to figure out she's secretly a mermaid. Along with Saltwater Souls, Hannah has also written The Atlantis Trilogy (published through SnowRidge Press), which contains even more mermaids, magic, and murder. Her short stories and award-winning flash fiction pieces have been published in various anthologies, including all of Twenty Hills's. She has also won Editor's Choice Award from Havok Publishing twice, for her pieces in the Prismatic and World Tour anthologies. In 2022, her flash fiction piece, "A Home for Nova," won a Realm Award. Hannah also won a competition with her short story, "Lara." In addition to fiction, she also has had over a dozen devotionals published in various magazines, as well as six devotions published in Finding God in Anime. In her spare time, she's probably either cuddling her cats, drinking tea, reading, or practicing for her imaginary Broadway debut. Connect with her on Instagram at @mermaidhannahwrites.

Miriam Wade is a Minnesota local who writes young adult fantasy, adventure, and urban fantasy driven by resilient young women, filled with twisty plots, and garnished with a hint of romance. She loves coffee, playing video games, and riding her bicycle. When she is not writing, she enjoys spending time with her husband, their two young daughters, and their cat. Wade is the author of the award-winning steampunk Arthurian inspired series, One Sword Saga, and the paranormal urban fantasy, The Woman of Blythe Manor, as well as a featured poet in several anthologies.

www.miriam-wade.com

@miriam.wade.author

www.facebook.com/miriam.wade.author

Ali Noël lives in the greater Seattle area with her three young kinds and rambunctious bulldog. If she's not writing or having a dance party, you can find her reading, baking or watching any take on a Jane Austen novel. Her work has been featured in *Z Publishing House, SobreMesa Zine* and *Wow! Women on Fiction.* You can find Ali and her poetry on Instagram @the.authoress.life

Brooke J. Katz is a stay at home/homeschooling mom by day and author/poet by night. Jesus and Lyons tea fuel her. Writing and painting have been a way for her to step into another world and for her work to be an outlet for someone else to find encouragement, or just some time to themselves being lost in a story. She is known to always have a book on her and dropping what she's doing to pray. You can find her on IG/Goodreads @Brookejkatz or her website

Rachel Lawrence writes from South Carolina, where she lives with her husband, four children, and no pets (despite the kids' constant campaign for one). She processes the world spinning around her and the thoughts swirling within her through stories and poetry. Her favorite poets range from King David to Elizabeth Barrett Browning to Taylor Swift. Her favorite Story is still being written.

Born and raised in South Africa, Maseeha Seedat takes inspiration for her stories from the most memorable moments of her life. She's a full-time student and a part-time writer, with her first novel, The Littlest Voices, published a year after her publishing debut with Twenty Hills. Her writing ranges from the fun and whimsical to the dark and serious, most of the time settling somewhere in the middle. When she's not writing, Maseeha can be found surrounded by her family and friends, or clawing her way toward a degree in physiotherapy.

When not writing or homeschooling her son, Crystal Bailey enjoys reading and watching old movies and television shows (The Golden Girls and I Love Lucy are her all-time favorites). Perusing antique stores for unique vintage finds, hiking with her family, and Jesus round out some of her other loves. She's unapologetically obsessed with all things post-apocalyptic or dystopian. Though she's called both Idaho and California home in the past, she now lives with her husband and son in the beautiful Texas Hill Country.

Elaine Wells is a young adult crazy cat lady, and an aspiring author with a poet's heart. Her poetry portrays her truth-seeking attitude. Some of her favorite poets include Edgar Allen Poe and Emily Dickinson, while drawing inspiration from Olivia Gatwood. She has a passion for writing about mental health, and she also loves photography, good books, deep conversations, and soft blankets.

Instagram @elaine.wells.poetry

Museum director by day and writer by night, Mary Agnes Ratelle is a lover of all things old, dusty, and antique. With a master's degree in art history and museum studies, Mary Agnes has a particular interest in historical fiction, immersing the reader in the aesthetics, culture, and complex issues of the past. When writing, Mary Agnes enjoys intersecting themes of faith, womanhood, family, and healing, hoping to come to a deeper understanding of the human person's greater purpose of love.

Morgan J. Manns is a speculative fiction writer who enjoys crafting enchanting worlds and captivating magic systems, a skill she nurtures after tucking her children into bed. Her imagination is fueled by the works of Brandon Sanderson, Patrick Rothfuss, and Samantha Shannon, serving as constant inspiration. By day, Morgan works as an English teacher, seeking ways to ignite the writing potential in her students while helping them uncover the transformative power of the written word. When she's not writing, or teaching about writing, she can be found chasing after her two young children, delving into fantasy novels alongside her husband, or exploring the breathtaking Canadian vistas surrounding her home. One of her favourite pastimes is canoeing with her family on the glistening lake just behind her house.

9 781956 499292